LIGHTNING STRIKES TWICE

A MARY BLAKE MYSTERY

AG BARNETT

ODDMOOR PRESS

MAILING LIST

Get FREE SHORT STORY *A Rather Inconvenient Corpse* by signing up to the mailing list at agbarnett.com

CHAPTER ONE

M ary looked around the space with a satisfied smile. Ok, it wasn't your usual sort of office. Your standard office tended not to have a snooker table as a desk. At least the chalk scoreboard was proving a useful way to keep track of notes. So far, the only thing written on it in large capital letters was 'GET CLIENTS!' but the point stood.

So far, in the three weeks, since they had announced to the world that they were starting a detective agency, they had received eighteen requests from people supposedly wanting help from the newly formed Blake, Blake and Tanner. Unfortunately, fourteen of these had proved to be fans of the hit crime show *Her Law*, in which Mary had played the lead role of Susan Law.

That part of Mary's life was over now. The tv

executives had decided that at the age of fifty, she was no longer an acceptable sight for the viewing public. A fact which had initially made her furious at the injustice of the world, but which had now cooled with time as she began to find a new life for herself.

This was in no small part due to the events that had taken place since her career had received such a fatal blow. The largest of which was undoubtedly the discovery of a long-lost family heirloom which had then been sold for a sum so huge; Mary still had to count the noughts each time she looked at her bank statement.

Although the discovery was the biggest in terms of national intrigue and journalistic appeal, two other events had made a far more significant impact in Mary's life. She had found herself embroiled in two separate murder cases and, along with her brother Pea and her old friend and further assistant Dot, had been integral to solving them both. The thrill, rush, and sense of accomplishment this had given her, surpassed anything else she had done in her entire life.

She had caught the bug of detection, a role she had played for so long on television, and yet had never dreamed of doing in real life. Now, with enough money to choose whatever path she wanted in life and a fierce determination to make it count.

She had started her own private detective agency. Well, along with Dot and Pea of course.

Once they had dismissed the fourteen enquiries from starstruck fans, they had dealt with the remaining four. Three had been missing person cases, all of whom had promptly turned up again before they could even get stuck in, and the last... the last was a local affair.

"I've got the pamphlet thingy," Pea said as he came through the door. She turned to see his tall frame striding across the old and threadbare carpet, his red hair flopped to one side and sticking out at varying points as it always seemed to. He was waving a small booklet in his left hand and held it out to Mary as he reached her. She took it from him and looked down at the front cover. On it, etched in black and white, was the outline of an Oak tree, its thick trunk split dramatically down the middle leaving a large oval hole at its centre. Above it, in gothic writing, were the words 'The Lightning Tree'. Her eyes drifted to the name at the bottom.

"It was written by Ethel Long?" Mary said, one eyebrow rising.

"Yep," Pea replied as he stretched his long arms and yawned, before flopping into an office chair that rolled backwards slightly. "Funny, I wouldn't have pegged her as an amateur historian."

"Maybe not," Mary agreed, "but this isn't exactly history is it? It's gossip and nonsense, something old Ethel Long excels at."

"Just because you don't understand it, don't dismiss it," Pea said.

Mary gave a small laugh and shook her head as she took a seat on the opposite side of the snooker table desk and opened the booklet. Inside was a brief description of the lightning tree and the legend surrounding it. Mary already knew the story; everyone who lived in the village of Bloxley or its surrounding areas did. Rural England is the kind of place that legends and myths thrive, and the North of the county of Adderbury was no different.

The tree, which dominated the village green at the village of Bloxley, had not always been known by such a dramatic name. It had once been known as The Giving Tree, a symbol of hope, rebirth, and fertility. It had been used in rituals that dated back to pagan times and had formed the centre of countless May Day ceremonies. Welcoming in the spring and all the hope and promise it brought for the local community of people who lived off the land.

Legend had it that a little under one hundred years ago a terrible storm swept across the rolling green hills, a storm like no one had ever seen. Fingers of lightning crept over the land as though seeking something, thunder rumbled and crashed as though the sky was splitting and the rain poured down in sheets that swelled the rivers for miles around.

The villagers battened down their windows and doors and hid in their houses until morning when it had blown itself out around dawn. They emerged blinking into a world of fallen branches, cracked tiles, and collapsed walls. None of this though had prepared them for what they had found at the village green.

The Giving Tree had been split by a violent bolt of pure energy that had cracked its old, gnarled trunk down the middle. Far worse though, was what lay on the floor of the newly created blackened hollow. A woman named Emily Blankforth, dead, from a vicious blow to her head.

Mary flicked through the pamphlet for a few moments as Pea browsed a magazine that had run a story on their new business.

"This is a great photo of you, Mary," he said, "it could have been taken right out of Her Law!"

"That's because it was," Mary answered, "They took it from a photoshoot I did a couple of years ago."

"Oh, right. Well, the article makes the new firm sound pretty exciting!"

"I think that's part of the problem," Mary answered, "no one's going to take it seriously after reading that. It sounds like we're making a new tv show."

Mary hadn't told the others, but this was truer than they knew. Her agent Terry had called her yesterday, furious that she had started talks on a new spin-off series without him.

"So," Mary said, deciding to bring matters back to the case in hand. "Ethel Long's theory on the original case is that Emily Blankforth wasn't a witch at all?"

"That's right," Pea answered, sitting upright, "caused quite a stir apparently when she put it out there. You know how much The Cauldron likes to big up the witch connection."

Mary smiled. The Cauldron, the village of Bloxley's only pub, enjoyed a central position in the village, at the back of the triangular village green. As the lightning tree dominated the pub's view, it made sense that thirty years ago, the then owners would have attempted to cash in on the legend. The pub had been renamed to The Cauldron from The Fox and had lined its walls with various objects of the occult. Sometimes, these objects were entirely devoid of magical overtones but were so strange looking or odd (like the vintage set of false teeth which stood in a small glass case on the mantelpiece), that they were deemed acceptable. It's six double bedrooms were similarly themed as 'spooky', which had the added ıan with a fire behind her eyes that often-caught ple off guard if they pushed her. Her father, a liant if a somewhat eccentric man, now spent his ys staring out of a window at a retirement home. is mind lost in a fog of tangled memories.

She remembered a family picnic, taken on the illage green at nearby Bloxley, underneath the ightning tree. Her father, animatedly telling the story of its legend as she and Pea rolled on the floor with laughter.

Something had happened to the lightning tree. It had been vandalised with a message that harked back to the past, and in particular, to witchcraft and murder.

benefit of reducing the amount of cleaning which pleased its landlord Frank Roach. Cobwebs only added to the authenticity.

"Well," Mary said with a sigh, "The Cauldron obviously have the most to gain, but Frank swears he had nothing to do with it. But the decision to ask us to look into it doesn't exactly scream innocence."

"What do you mean?" Pea blinked at her. "Why would Frank ask us to look into it if he'd vandalised the tree himself?"

Mary rolled her eyes.

"You better not be this dim in front of clients you know. He'd do it for the publicity! Think about it. We announce we're starting a private detective agency and get a bit of press. What better way to drum up business for the pub than to have a real-life mystery outside that drags us in?"

"I see," Pea said thoughtfully. "Good point." His slightly receding brow furrowed.

"You really need to start being more cynical," Mary said, shaking her head and standing. "Come on, Dot's train should be getting in soon, let's pick her up and go and look at this bloody tree."

As Mary walked across the former snooker room of her family home at Blancham hall, her mind drifted to her childhood in the large and slightly crumbling building. Her mother, a smiling, kind woman with a fire behind her eyes that often-caught people off guard if they pushed her. Her father, a brilliant if a somewhat eccentric man, now spent his days staring out of a window at a retirement home. His mind lost in a fog of tangled memories.

She remembered a family picnic, taken on the village green at nearby Bloxley, underneath the lightning tree. Her father, animatedly telling the story of its legend as she and Pea rolled on the floor with laughter.

Something had happened to the lightning tree. It had been vandalised with a message that harked back to the past, and in particular, to witchcraft and murder.

CHAPTER TWO

The station at Bloxley was little more than a raised stone platform alongside the tracks and a small wooden shelter that leaned precariously to one side. As it had tilted like this since she had been a child, Mary held no fear that it would collapse any time soon. She picked at the peeling blue paint.

"We should spruce this place up a bit," she said to Pea as her eye scanned the weeds which had forced their way through the cracked and broken brickwork.

"I've been meaning to talk to you about that," Pea said, leaning out over the track and peering down the line towards Tanbury, from which direction Dot's train would arrive.

"You think we should write to the train company?" Mary asked, "I doubt they'd be interested. It's a miracle the trains still stop here as it is."

The horn of a train rang out in the distance.

"Here she comes!" Pea said, his cheeks reddening.

Mary couldn't help but smile. Her brother and her best friend were in the early stages of a romance that seemed to have turned them into teenagers. Well, Pea at least. Dot had indeed shown uncharacteristic signs of soppiness, but they were just small cracks in her general business-like demeanour compared to the full puppy dog look that Pea seemed to have whenever she was around.

Mary's smile faded slightly as her thoughts drifted to her own love life: or lack of one. She still got messages from old flames asking her out to dinner or a show in London, but she'd stopped that side of life almost as abruptly as her acting career had been cut short. She hadn't just lost her job; she had lost her identity. Now, she was rebuilding it, but what that meant for her love life, she had yet to figure out. Inspector Joe Corrigan rose into her mind as he always seemed to these days. She shook him clear from her mind as the train pulled to a stop, and Dot stepped down from the third carriage.

"Hello!" Pea said enthusiastically, helping her

down the small step to the platform and kissing her on the cheek. "How was the journey? Ok?"

"Fine, thank you," Dot said, "only a half-hour delay which is better than usual."

Pea took her suitcase from her as Mary gave her a welcoming hug.

"Good to have you back, Dot. Pea was driving me mad, I need a buffer."

Dot Tanner laughed but then gave Mary a slightly disapproving look at being referred to as a buffer.

"Well, everything's in hand in London. So I can stay for a while."

"Great!" Pea exclaimed, then looked sheepish at the outburst. "I'll just get this in the car." He turned and wheeled the suitcase towards the small car park.

"He's been pining after you like a lovesick puppy," Mary said in a low voice as she linked her arm through Dot's and followed.

"Don't be silly, Mary."

"I'm serious! If you were going to take any longer in London, I was going to send him up to you to get rid of him!"

Dot tutted, but Mary saw the smile on her face.

"We're not going straight to the Hall I'm afraid, we have a case!"

"What is it this time?" Dot said sharply. "Someone wants you to sign a poster or something?"

"No! It's a real one! Well, sort of."

"What do you mean by 'sort of'?"

"I think it's best we take a look at it and go from there," Mary answered as they reached the car where Pea held open the front passenger door for Dot.

Mary climbed into the back seat, realising that this was now her place in the group. She was the third wheel.

"Come on, don't keep me in suspense. What is it?" Dot asked as Pea pulled the car out of the parking space.

"Someone's defaced the lightning tree," Pea answered in a dramatic voice.

"That old, dead tree in the village?"

"It's not dead," Pea corrected, "it's still alive even with the split in the trunk. Amazingly hardy things, trees."

"So," Dot said with a sigh. "Village vandalism. I can't imagine this is going to pay very much, who's asked us to look into it?"

"Frank Roach," Mary answered from the back, "he's the landlord at the cauldron, and it's a bit more than just village vandalism."

"What do you mean?"

"You'll see," Mary answered as they rounded the

sharp bend that turned into the village of Bloxley. The warm coloured stone buildings topped with thatch crowded the short, narrow lane which opened out to the village green.

"There it is," Pea said as he pulled the car alongside the large triangular grass area, the lightning tree at its centre.

"Bloody hell," Mary said in shock. "Whoever did this wasn't messing about were they?"

They climbed out of the car and walked across the still-damp grass towards the tree in silence. All three of their gazes, locked onto the writing burnt into its trunk.

"How on earth did they do that?" Dot asked, squinting up at it.

"With a ladder, unless they were ten-foot-tall," Pea answered.

"I don't mean how high it is, I mean burn the letters in like that?"

"They must have used some kind of accelerant," Mary said confidently, using a line she had used on her tv show numerous times.

"Tree bark isn't as easy to set on fire when it's still on the tree," Pea added, "once the stuff they'd put on had burnt off it would have just fizzled out."

"What does it mean?" Dot asked.

Mary and Pea exchanged glances.

"I think," Mary answered slowly, "that rather depends on how much you believe in legends."

She looked back up at the writing that was crudely burnt into the side of the tree that still maintained the integrity of its trunk.

1 MORE WITCH

CHAPTER THREE

"Come on, Frank," Pea said, leaning on the bar of the cauldron pub. "Are you sure this isn't just some publicity stunt?"

Mary glanced at him, impressed with how quickly he had absorbed this point of view as his own.

"I'm telling you," Frank answered, "I know nothing about it!"

Frank Roach was a portly figure with a slick, teddy boy haircut despite the receding hairline. His thin moustache and black silk shirt were adding to the sense that he had just time travelled from a dance hall in the nineteen fifties.

"I mean, it's going to be bloody good for business, that's why I got a photo over to the gazette sharpish, but I wouldn't want someone doing that to the tree. It's not right, is it?"

"It happened right outside," Mary chimed in. "Are you telling me you didn't hear or see anything?"

"No! They must have done it in the middle of the night. I didn't close up until..." He hesitated.

Pea realised that Frank's license only allowed him to serve alcohol until eleven o'clock at night.

"Ha! Don't be ridiculous, Frank," Pea said laughing, "we've been at enough of your lock-ins for you to know it's fine and we're not police."

"Right, well," Frank said, leaning back and shrugging his shoulders, "we had some of the regulars in, and we were all 'having a good old natter about the to-do we had in here last week, so it ran a little late. Anyway, everyone who was here says nothing was happening at the tree when they walked home."

"And what time was that?" Mary asked, somewhat impatiently.

"Must have been about one?"

"Any chance you could write a list of who was in here until then?" Mary said as she pulled a small notebook from her pocket and slid it across the bar along with a ballpoint pen. Trying not to be self-conscious about how shiny it's black cover was, it was clearly unused.

"All right," Frank grumbled, taking the pad and

pen, "but I doubt any of those reprobates will be able to help you. Whoever did this is an outsider."

"What makes you say that?" Pea asked, his voice rising in excitement.

"What the bloody hell would anyone living in Bloxley do it for?" he said, looking up from the pad. "We've all lived here for years, hardly likely one of us is going to set fire to the bloody thing suddenly."

"And what about the message?" Mary asked as the landlord turned back to his notebook. "What do you think it means?"

Frank finished the last name and pushed the pad back across the bar.

"What it means?" He replied blinking. "Bloody obvious what it means isn't it?! It's saying there's another witch in the village, and you know what happened to the last one."

Mary looked at her brother, who returned her look of confusion with one of excitement.

"You mean this is history repeating itself?" he garbled excitedly. "That there's another witch in the village and the lightning tree is going to claim her like it did poor Emily Blankforth?!"

Mary rolled her eyes.

"For goodness sake Pea, of course, he doesn't!"

She shook her head as she laughed and looked back to Frank. He was staring back at her with a stone-faced expression of utter seriousness. Slowly, one eyebrow rose.

"You can't be serious?!" Mary said, looking between the two men as Pea shrugged.

"Come on, Mary, it's got to be related."

"Like some kind of prank, yes, but there's no bloody witch in the village!"

"We'll soon find out if the lightning tree gets its way," Frank nodded sagely.

"Exactly," Pea agreed with enthusiasm.

"You said that people here were talking about something that had happened last week?" Mary asked, trying to bring the conversation back to some kind of reality.

Frank's eyes darted around the pub, despite it being empty. "Yeah, well, things have been a bit heated around here recently. There was a bit of a scuffle here last week."

"Who was it?"

"It wasn't much of anything really, nothing to worry you about."

Mary folded her arms, her eyes narrowing.

"Why exactly are you willing to pay for us to look into this?"

Frank looked between us, his brow furrowing. "Not good for the village is it? Not if people are going around and doing things like that."

"Might be good for business though," Mary said, "like Pea said, this does smack of a publicity stunt."

Frank sighed. "Fine, I thought getting you involved would maybe get the pub some cheap publicity, but I had nothing to do with that out there." He gestured towards the front of the pub.

"Right," Mary said, still glaring, "at least we now know where we both stand."

"So, about this witch," Pea continued, leaning one elbow on the bar.

Mary rolled her eyes and turned back towards the front door of the pub, leaving Pea andFrank discussing the finer points of witchcraft.

They had left Dot out on the green, reading through the pamphlet Pea brought earlier. She had done so with more enthusiasm than Mary, as the entire tale was new to her. She had sat on one of the two benches that flanked the tree and told them to go on ahead.

Now, as Mary emerged from the gloom of the pub, she saw the stocky figure of her old friend looking up at the tree, one hand shedding her eyes.

"So, what do you make of our little legend?" she said as she crossed the grass towards her.

"Well I think the version in this makes more sense than the woman being a witch," Dot said, waving the pamphlet.

"Tell that to my brother and that idiot landlord," Mary answered, "they're both convinced this means there's another witch in the village that's going to suffer the same fate as Emily Blankforth."

Mary had expected Dot to reply with a cutting comment about how foolish they were being, but instead, there was silence. She turned to her as Dot took a deep breath.

"Maybe they're right?" she said as she exhaled.

"You can't be serious," Mary said, laughing. "Bloody hell Dot, a few days in my brother's company, and he's got you believing in witches and magic!"

"No, I don't mean that," Dot said dismissively. "I mean, what if this is a warning to someone? What if someone is threatening someone else by suggesting they might suffer the same fate as that poor woman?"

Mary blinked and looked up into the dark hollow which rose from the base of the wide trunk and ran upwards towards the branches.

"Then we should find out if anyone around here has been called a witch before," she said quietly, "and there's one person who knows everything in this village."

CHAPTER FOUR

E thel Long was the kind of character that every village in England seemed to have. Call them what you like, a busybody, a nosey parker, a gossip. Whatever label you gave them, they acted in the same way. They thrived on rumour, on tittle-tattle, and loved nothing more than to pass on anything and everything they had heard.

Despite this, Ethel Long was still the person that people in the village went to, to get things off their chest. For one thing, she always had the best gossip about everyone else in the village. All you had to do to tease it out of her was to give a little of your own, something that had become of use in certain situations for the villagers of Bloxley. If someone had, for instance, had a poor piece of meat from George Copeland, the butcher. A discreet word to Ethel that his standards had slipped was sure to be around the village in days. Which would have poor George throwing away anything that wasn't top quality no matter how it ate into his profits.

"So good to see you!" Ethel smiled as Mary stepped into the low-ceilinged hallway of her stone cottage. "I can't even begin to think about how long it's been!"

"Quite a while, Ethel, yes," Mary answered, smiling. "How have you been keeping?"

"Oh, you know, can't complain. Not like old Mrs Parchment, I imagine you've heard all about what's happened there?"

"No?" Mary answered as she followed the woman through to her small and cluttered front room. Feeling glad she had instructed Dot and Pea to head back to Blancham Hall to catch up; she wasn't sure they would have all fit into the cramped space.

"Let me fetch you some tea, and I'll tell you all about it!" Ethel grinned, her thin face alive with pleasure at having a new audience for her gossip. She disappeared through a doorway into the kitchen beyond, and Mary looked around the room.

Every surface lay covered in ornaments and photographs. Small china figures of various animals stood dotted across a lace throw that draped over a sideboard. A dresser stood against one wall and contained porcelain figures of dancers as well as pictures. The bottom shelf was of grinning grandchildren and family groups, all smiles. The images higher up were scenes of Bloxley, some dating back to when Ethel would have been a child. In the middle of the top shelf, was a large black and white picture of the lightning tree.

A few moments later, Ethel had returned and launched into the details of Mrs Parchment's hip replacement that had become infected and caused her to have a lengthy stay in hospital. Entirely how Ethel knew so many of the medical details, Mary was unsure. Guesswork seemed to be the most likely answer. On a roll, Ethel then continued to explain how Charles Cotton, who ran the post office, had been seen drinking too much in the Cauldron and that things might not be right at home. His wife Gloria had apparently been snappy with customers recently. When she moved on to how many ladies of the village having a crush on the new vicar, Mary decided it was time to reign her in and get her back on track.

"So, what do you make of what's happened to the lightning tree?"

Ethel's eyes glinted with pleasure as a smile crept across her thin lips. She had the look of a spider whose web had just caught a particularly juicy fly.

"I thought that might be why you're here," she said as she placed her teacup on the table next to her and leaned forward from her wing-backed armchair. "Someone's trying to make a point, don't you think?"

"Maybe," Mary answered noncommittally, "it could just be kids messing around?"

"Ha!" Ethel snorted. "There aren't any kids in Bloxley anymore! Well, a few little nippers, but when they grow up a bit, they'll soon leave. Nothing here for them."

"You think this was someone making a threat?"

"No better place to do it." Ethel shrugged, her smile widening. "The whole village saw that within a half-hour of the sun going up."

"But who do you think they could be threatening? Who around here would people think of as a witch?"

Ethel cackled loudly, causing her to cough. She pulled a handkerchief from her sleeve and dabbed at her mouth as she regained her composure.

"I'm the only one they call witch around here!" She laughed. "Though I doubt that's meant for me. Have you read my pamphlet on the lightning tree?"

"I have, you don't think Emily Blankforth was a witch?"

"Of course, she wasn't!" Ethel laughed again.

"She was just a young girl who'd had her head turned and loosened her skirts where she shouldn't have."

"And you think that's what's happening here?"

"People are always the same," Ethel said, wagging a finger at her. "They might moan about this and that, but there are only two things that ever make them do something drastic, lust and money. You mark my words."

Mary studied the thin, wrinkled face of the woman before her with newfound respect. She had always considered Ethel to be a shallow purveyor of gossip. Now, she was getting the impression she may well have been a better study of human character than that.

"Who do you think, did it? Who do you think it's about?"

Ethel's eyes glistened. "I have my thoughts, and I'll make sure everyone sees sense about the whole thing."

Mary frowned. "I'm sorry, I don't follow?"

The doorbell rang out, and Ethel stood up quickly. "Sorry Mary, but I've got a lot of visitors coming today with everything that's happened, so if you wouldn't mind?" She gestured towards the door.

Mary stood up, feeling as though she was being dismissed from a tv audition that had gone badly and followed her down the hallway to the front door. She was met by a middle-aged woman in a long wax coat, which bulged in various places to hold her ample frame.

"Hello Gloria, good to see you," Ethel said. "Mary here was just leaving."

Mary and Gloria Cotton, who ran the village shop and post office with her husband Charles, said a quick hello before Ethel hurried her into the house and closed the door behind them.

"Charming," Mary muttered as she turned to head down the small garden path and walked straight into a short, stocky woman with greying brown hair in a neat bob.

"Oh, I'm sorry," she muttered before looking up, and a look of realisation passed across her face.

"Mary!"

"Hello Beryl, how are you?"

"Oh, yes, fine, fine." Her narrow eyes darted between her and the door behind. "Just been to see Ethel have you?"

"Yes, are you visiting?"

"Um, yes. I like to check in," she said. "You know, in case she needs anything from the shop I could bring around for her."

Beryl Copeland ran the butchers shop with her husband George. Mary pictured Ethel Long in her mind. If there was one label, she could have given her; it would be spry.

"She doesn't seem like she needs much help to me," Mary said.

Beryl laughed, but it was an uneasy one. "You're right enough there, but it's the thought that counts. Nice to see you. Mary."

She began to move past her towards the door.

"Gloria Cotton is in there at the moment," Mary called after her. "She watched her hesitate then stop. She had guessed right. Whatever Beryl had to gossip about with Ethel Long, she wanted to say do in private.

"Perhaps I'll pop back later," she said, turning and hurrying back down the path towards her.

"Were you and George in the pub last night?" Mary said as she followed her out onto the small road that ran along one side of the village green and out into the countryside.

"George was, why?" Beryl said, turning back to Mary with her round face pinched in suspicion. Then her eyes widened in understanding. "Oh, because of what happened with the lightning tree? Awful business. George didn't see anything if that's what you're after. I hear you're looking into it for Frank?"

"Word travels fast," Mary said with a small laugh.

"Yes, well. You can't keep anything private in this village," she said, with a tight smile. "Give my regards to your brother, Mary."

Mary watched her go and pulled out her phone to call Pea for a lift home.

CHAPTER FIVE

"Well, we didn't get anywhere," Pea said as he took another large sip of red wine. "The police have put it down to kids messing around obviously, and the local paper is going down the witchcraft route."

"They aren't the only ones," Mary said, raising an eyebrow at him.

"Don't worry," Dot said firmly, "I've told him he's being ridiculous." The firmness of her tone forcing Pea into a sheepish expression.

"What is the Gazette saying?" Mary asked.

"They're saying that witchcraft has come to Bloxley once again!" Pea said enthusiastically, eyebrows waggling. "They're going to send someone down to cover events on the ground, staying at the cauldron."

Mary sighed. "Well, no prizes for guessing who's orchestrated that. Frank must be rubbing his hands at getting the Cauldron as the centre of attention. I still think he's our best bet for having done this."

"Oh, come on, Mary," Pea countered, "you heard him. He says he had nothing to do with it."

"You really are too gullible by far, you know." Mary laughed.

"Yes, he is, have you told Mary about that investment opportunity of yours?"

Pea reddened. "Look, come on Dot. You don't know that anything's wrong with it. These things take time."

"What's this?" Mary asked with concern.

"It's nothing," Pea said with a wave of his hand.

Before Mary could ask anything further, Hetty bustled in, pushing a trolley laden with food.

"How did the chops work out, Hetty?" Pea said cheerily, welcome of the distraction.

"They took some cajoling, but I think I've got them under control." She laughed. "And how was George Copeland when you bought them?"

"Grumpy," Pea answered, his eyes following the dishes of food as they were laid out before them.

"No change there then!" Hetty huffed. "Whole bloody village has gone loopy if you ask me."

"What do you mean?" Mary asked.

"I've never known the place like it!" Hetty continued. "Everyone getting all hot and bothered over nothing, fights in the pub. Some sort of madness it is."

"You're saying the villagers are getting restless?" Pea said as he shovelled food onto his plate.

"The villagers are getting restless?" Mary parroted. "You're not Count Dracula."

"What's got everyone all riled up then?" Dot asked as Hetty took a seat to her right.

"No idea! I asked Beryl when I saw her in the post office, but she just looked at me all funny and made some excuse about having to do some stock-taking! I mean, have you ever known anyone in this village to miss an opportunity to natter?!"

"Actually," Mary said thoughtfully, "now I think about it, Frank said something about things being heated in the village recently."

"And that was before all this business with the lightning tree," Hetty added. "Ethel Long's door hasn't stopped flapping all day!"

"That's who you went to see isn't it Mary? This Ethel Long?" Dot asked.

"Did you?!" Hetty said excitedly. "What did she say?"

"Not much." Mary shrugged. "Then again, she hadn't spoken to half the village when I'd spoken to her. She's probably got all the gossip on it all by now."

"Then you'll just have to go and see her again," Dot said firmly. "Maybe, Hetty," she continued, "it would be a good idea if you told us what all this tension in the village has looked like? What's actually been happening?"

"Well, of course, I'm not one for spreading rumours," Hetty began, causing Mary and Pea to exchange knowing glances, "but Gloria and Charles were in the middle of a right old ding-dong in the shop went I went in the other day."

"What about?" Mary asked.

"I don't know," Hetty said, waving her fork dismissively before she attacked another roast potato. "They clammed up as soon as I came in. Anyway, then there was all this fuss at the pub last weekend."

"You heard about that?" Pea asked in a rare moment when his mouth wasn't full.

"Heard about it? I was there!"

"Come on then, spill the beans!"

"Well, the shocking thing is, it was the new vicar that was in the middle of it all!"

"The vicar was in a pub fight?!" Dot said, her usually calm exterior vanishing in an instant.

"He wasn't exactly throwing punches or

anything, but he was at the centre of it all right! It all started when he was talking to George Copeland."

"The local butcher," Pea said to Dot, who nodded in response.

"Suddenly George flew right off the handle and started shouting and swearing and all sorts!"

"At the vicar?!" Dot said in shock, her food now forgotten.

"Yes!" Hetty cried, "Bold as brass! Mind you, he did seem to have had a skinful. So, of course, I tried to step in."

"Hetty Wainthropp," Pea said, continuing to fill Dot in with a smile on his lips. "Local woman, sticks her nose in everything that happens in the village."

Hetty glared at him and Pea jumped in his seat and clutched his leg where she'd kicked him.

"Then," Hetty continued, "the Cotton's got in the middle of it all, and George whacked the vicar right on the nose!"

"Blimey!" Pea said, before turning to Dot again. "The Cottons run the local shop."

"Lilly Cooper was there and got her glass of wine knocked right down her front!" Hetty chortled, wiping a tear from her eye. "Anyway, Frank split them all up and kicked them out before things got any more out of hand."

"He kicked the vicar out?!"

"Bloody hell, Dot, can we get over the vicar already?" Mary said as she laid her cutlery together on the plate and leaned back in her chair. "It sounds like we need to speak to everyone who was there. I doubt it's got anything to do with the damage to the lightning tree, but it's worth a try."

"Oh, that has nothing to do with the lightning tree," Hetty said dismissively.

"How can you be so sure?"

Hetty put down her cutlery and turned to Mary with a grim expression etched on her rounded face.

"Everyone in the village on edge? A message about a witch burnt into the lightning tree? There's something dark going on around here, mark my words. We all know what happened all those years ago."

"Hetty!" Mary cried exasperated. "Not you as well!"

"All I'm saying is, you can't explain what's been happening in the village, and you can't tell me someone climbed a ladder in the middle of the night and burnt the tree without anyone seeing?!"

"Of course they did! What? Do you think it was some evil spirits or something?!"

"All I'm saying is that it's all a bit funny," Hetty said huffily.

"Well, I'm with you Hetty," Pea said. Dot raised

an eyebrow at him. "Don't look at me like that!" Pea laughed. "There's nothing wrong in believing in a bit of magic!"

Mary retired early. The doe-eyed looks between her brother and Dot had reached uncomfortable levels. With Hetty heading back to the village, she felt in danger of feeling like a third wheel.

She had taken a large whiskey on the rocks to her room and was standing at the window, staring out at the distant lights of Bloxley through the driving rain. Thunder rumbled in the distance, and her thoughts turned to the Lightning Tree.

Why would anyone deface it? What would motivate someone to creep out in the middle of the night with a step-ladder and some way of burning letters into the trunk of the old tree? She had no idea, but it would take a lot.

She took another swig of whiskey as a bad feeling rose in her gut. Dot was right. Whoever had done this was trying to send a message and the only thing she was sure of, was that it wasn't a pleasant one. She watched lightning flash across the sky in the distance and drained her drink.

CHAPTER SIX

M ary woke to a frantic banging on her bedroom door.

"Bloody hell!" She moaned as she rolled away from the noise and pulled the bedcovers over her head. "Go away!"

"There's been a murder, Mary!" Pea's voice called urgently through the thick oak doors that were standard throughout Blancham Hall. She sat upright, her mind attempting to shake off the fuzziness of sleep and focus on what she had just heard.

A murder.

She jumped out of bed and ran across to the door, unlocking it and throwing it open. Pea was standing wide-eyed; his red hair tousled on top of his head as though he'd just stepped out if a wind tunnel, his pale blue pyjamas hanging from his thin frame.

"A murder, Mary!" he repeated. "I don't know who it is yet, but the body was in the lightning tree!"

"Get dressed; we need to get down there now, and wake Dot up."

Pea grinned sheepishly. "She's already awake."

"Right," Mary said flatly. She decided that to enquire further would too much information to a wakeup call that had involved murder and so instead closed the door quickly and hurried to get dressed.

It was only twenty minutes later when Pea was edging the old Rolls Royce through the country lanes the short distance towards the village. The car, having languished in the garage for decades, had finally been restored at considerable expense by Pea, who considered it a family heirloom. Luckily, their newfound fortune was more than enough to indulge in such frivolities.

The scene when they reached the village was one of complete chaos. A muddle of police and press were gathered outside the Cauldron pub, each group keeping very carefully to its own, but eyeing each other suspiciously. In front of the tree itself was a white tent. Erected so that one end wrapped around the lightning tree and hid its famous hollow, and presumably the corpse inside, from view.

"Bloody hell," Pea said as he pulled the car to a stop in one of the last available spaces still available at the edge of the grass. "It must be a bad one. This is a lot of fuss."

"You tend to get that when someone's been killed," Dot said coldly as they all stepped out of the car.

Mary's heart fluttered in her chest as she spotted Inspector Joe Corrigan emerging from the tent. Her eyes had been searching for him from the moment the car had pulled into the centre of the village, but now she saw him, she felt unprepared. So far, their relationship had consisted of arguing during two murder cases that Mary had somehow become embroiled in, and a couple of rather awkward dates. What confused Mary more than anything was the awkwardness she felt in his presence. He rattled her, annoyed her, confused her. This wasn't Mary. She had always been calm, confident, in control. These new feelings both excited and frightened her in equal measure.

The three of them followed the road to their left, heading towards the small crowd at the pub, as Pea talked excitedly about witches in a low voice. Mary concentrated on the cracked and worn tarmac of the road, but even so, she could feel his eyes burning into the side of her head even before he called out to her.

"I might have known!" His voice rang out; it's deep tone causing Mary to stop in her tracks. She took a deep breath and turned slowly. He was walking across the green towards them in dark blue chinos a white shirt and a blue jumper. Mary fought against the smile that was trying to manifest itself on her face.

"It seems like it's impossible to discover a body around here without finding you nearby, isn't it?" Corrigan said.

Mary shrugged and stared back at him.

"I wonder," he continued, "if I should start just automatically adding you to the suspect list in murder cases? It might save me some time; I could just keep your file handy." It was his turn to shrug as he stopped in front of her, his blue eyes twinkling in the morning light as a smile played on his lips.

"Is this what passes for humour in the Adderbury police force?" Mary answered, folding her arms. "No wonder you all look so serious all the time. So, are you going to tell us what you've got so far?"

"You know I'm not supposed to share details of an ongoing case," he answered.

"That's ok; I'd imagine the villagers are better informed than your lot in any case."

Before he could answer, she turned away towards the pub and strode past Dot and Pea who moved to follow her. Pea flashed a sheepish grin at Corrigan, while Dot was as impassive as ever. Still, both were clearly relieved to get away from the awkward conversation.

There was a murmur from the small group of the press as she approached. Although she had been dumped by the production company that made *Her Law*, the media hadn't yet been able to let her go as one of the nation's darlings. What they had done, was to paint her as a sad tale of a career that had run its course. Something that annoyed her more than she cared to admit.

"Mary!" Shouted a pasty looking man with blonde hair. He scurried across to her while removing the lens cap from the large camera that was hanging from his neck. "What do you know about the victim?"

"Nothing at all," Mary replied, "I just live here and want to make sure the community I'm part of is safe."

"Do you think this is to do with you setting up a detective agency here in the last week?" shouted another voice.

"I really think," said a loud and high toned male voice, "that we should give Miss Blake time to acclimatise, don't you?"

Mary looked to the right of the press group and saw a young man who seemed instantly familiar to her. He gave a thin smile and tilted his head to one side in a gesture that indicated they should talk elsewhere as he moved away from the rest of the group. Mary moved back towards the green behind him as she heard Pea and Dot fielding the rest of the press's questions behind her.

"You broke into the grounds of my home," Mary said when he stopped and turned back to her.

"Purely in the interests of journalism I assure you," the man answered.

He was of a slender build and no more than late twenties in age. He had sharp, intelligent eyes and a pointed chin which added to his arrogant air.

Mary recognised him as the man who had been on the grounds of her family home, Blancham Hall, during the first murder enquiry she had been embroiled in. He had been near the folly by the lake where she had discovered the clue which would lead them to find the long lost Faberge egg which had made her and her brother Pea rich beyond reason. She had later realised that he, too, had found that clue, but had been unable to uncover the next. Mary had often thought about what might have happened had he discovered it before her.

"What are you doing here?" she said, arms folded, defiance in her voice.

"Us journalists always follow a good story," he

smiled, "and I think there's a particularly juicy one brewing here."

"Are you really a journalist?

"I try to find out things," the man answered with a light tone, "and I find I'm rather good at it."

"You didn't find out where the Faberge egg was," Mary retorted. "How did you even know it existed?!"

"As I said, I'm good at finding out things," he answered, his tone somewhat colder now. "Which is why I know who that is they've found in the tree over there." He jerked his back towards where the crime scene tent was erected against the Lightning tree. "I also know that you visited them yesterday, and it got me wondering what a coincidence it is that you always seem to be around these suspicious deaths. What is it? Three now?"

Mary wasn't listening. Her mind still stuck on his first point. "It's Ethel Long," she said in a quiet voice.

"And finally she gets it," the man laughed, "by the way, my name is Matt Sharpe. I'm sure you'll b hearing a lot more of me."

He turned and walked away.

"Who was that?" Dot asked as she and Pea joined her.

Mary took a deep breath. "That was a man named Matt Sharpe, and I don't think I like him at all. We've got more important things to worry about now though, like the fact that it's Ethel Long lying in that tree."

"The woman you went to see yesterday?" Dot asked.

"Along with half the village according to Hetty," Pea said, before giving a low whistle and adding, "bloody hell."

"Poor Ethel. This case just got personal. Come on, let's go and catch up with the locals." They turned back towards the pub.

The media had all scurried off to one side where they were eagerly taking a statement from Corrigan. Who's unreadable expression gave the Mary impression he was giving nothing away. To their right, the small gathering of locals muttered in low voices, their eyes all turned to the rear of the Lightning Tree.

"Mary, Percy," Frank Roach nodded at them as he separated himself from the group and met them as they approached. His eyes fell on Dot and lingered there for a moment. "I'm sorry, I don't think we've met?" He held out a hand, and Dot offered hers, only to be surprised when Frank bent and kissed it.

"My name is Dot Tanner," she answered in a slightly shocked tone.

"Charmed," franks said with a grin.

"Steady on," Pea muttered, his cheeks glowing as his eyes darted between them.

"What's going on, Frank?" Mary asked. Is it really Ethel Long they've found?"

Frank released Dot's hand, his face turning serious.

"Yep. Charles found her this morning when he was out walking the dog. Just laid right in the hollow she was, covered in blood." He turned to Pea. "Course, you know what they're saying, don't you?"

Pea's eyes widened. "You think this is the old curse coming back! Ethel was the witch the message was about?!"

"Oh, for goodness sake," Mary said, punching her brother on the arm, "will you stop going on about witchcraft. Frank, where is Charles now?" She asked, glancing over his shoulder at the small group of locals gathered behind him and not seeing the village shop owner Charles Cotton among them.

"Went home with an officer. The dog was going bloody crazy."

"Did he say anything else about what he saw?"

Frank's eyes fixed on her, their narrowed darkness reflecting the slicked-back quiff atop his head. "He said there were symbols on her."

Mary frowned, ignoring the gasp from Pea to her left. "What do you mean symbols?"

"I mean symbols," Frank said with a meaningful widening of his eyes. "Occult symbols, drawn all over her body in chalk. Her eyes were open as well. Charles said it was like she died of fright right there in the tree."

"Apart from all the blood?" Dot said in an annoyed tone.

"Sorry?" Frank blinked.

"You said that she was covered in blood earlier, which doesn't seem likely from just dying of fright."

"No, true," Frank said, smiling at her. "You're quite a feisty one, aren't you?" He winked at her, and Mary felt Pea bristle beside her.

"Maybe we should go and see if we can talk to Charles," Pea said firmly.

"Not before I talk to Corrigan properly," Mary sighed, turning to where the inspector, finished with the press, was walking towards them.

"Can I have a word, Miss Blake?" He said formally while the reporters were still in earshot, his face blank and unreadable.

Mary nodded, and they walked onto the grass of the village green, stopping halfway to the Lightning Tree at its centre.

"Who was that reporter you were talking to earlier?" Corrigan said, his tone curt and businesslike.

"Reporter?" Mary answered, momentarily thrown by the question before realising who he meant. "Oh, that cocky so-and-so Matt Sharpe?"

"What paper does he work for?"

"How should I know?!"

"What did he want?"

"Look," Mary said, getting angry, "would you mind doing me the courtesy of telling me what the hell is going on? Why do you care who he was?"

Corrigan sighed, his dark brown eyes looking to the heavens. "One of my men has just found out that this," he waved his hand as though trying to remember, "Matt Sharpe, was here on the scene early and got a photo."

"And you've let him walk away with it," Mary said grinning.

"It's not funny Mary. If that picture gets out we're going to have half the country's news teams bearing down on us."

Mary frowned for a moment before catching up to speed. "You mean because of the symbols that were drawn on Ethel?"

He looked at her sharply, then closed his eyes and swore quietly under his breath. "So that's going to be all over the press already as well then. Bloody villages. You can never keep a lid on anything."

"She was hit over the head, right?" Mary asked.

He sighed before answering. "Looks like it. We've got no murder weapon and no physical evidence to speak of due to the rain last night. On top of that, there's this bloody witchcraft stuff which I just know is going to complicate matters. Anything you can tell me about the place?"

"Not much to tell." Mary shrugged. "It's a small village. Normally everyone knows everything that's going on, but this message being burnt into the tree seems to have thrown everyone. Now, this."

"Do you think the two incidents are related?"

"Hard to see how they can't be," she answered, "happening within a day of each other like this, but why would anyone do it? It makes no sense!"

"You can't think of a reason why anyone would want to kill Ethel Long?"

"No, not really," she answered slowly, then caught his enquiring look. "She's a bit of a gossip." She shrugged and then noted her mistake. "Was a bit of a gossip, but that was just harmless village stuff, nothing that would have caused someone to do this."

"What might seem like harmless gossip to one person, might be considered dangerous to another," Corrigan said darkly. "I better go and find this bloody reporter; I don't suppose you know who he works for?"

"Not a clue," Mary answered truthfully. She

considered mentioning that the same reporter had been present at the first murder case they had both been part of, but Corrigan had already begun walking away.

"I don't suppose there's any point in me telling you to stay out of it?" He called over his shoulder.

"None at all," Mary answered.

The chuckle she heard him give made her heart beat a little faster.

CHAPTER SEVEN

"I told you," Pea said, "there could be some witchcraft mixed up in all this after all! Symbols were drawn all over the body. Must be something to do with making an offering to the devil.

"So now we've got devil worship going on in Bloxley as well as witchcraft?" Mary said with a sigh.

"All the same thing isn't it?" Pea answered before adopting a booming theatrical tone, "Dark occult things far beyond the understanding of mortal men!"

"Don't be an idiot," Dot said sharply, "that's obviously what whoever did this *wants* you to think."

"But why would anyone want to make us think that. "

"To create confusion and hide the actual motive," Mary answered exasperatedly.

"Which is?" Pea asked.

"How the bloody hell should I know?!" Mary said, waving her arms and stopping in the road.

They had been walking down one of the small lanes of the village that ran out from the green. Dodging the large puddles that were still gathered from the rain of two days ago.

Their destination, the Post Office, was in sight now. Its faded blue and white striped awning flapping gently in the still gusting breeze. Usually, a sign stood out on the pavement showing the latest headlines from the Gazette, but it was absent today. Presumably because Charles Cotton had had other things on his mind when he had returned home from his dog walk that morning. Mary thought back to when she had seen his wife yesterday. Arriving at Ethel Long's house, as so many other villagers had done, after the shocking defacement of the Lightning Tree.

She stopped on the pavement, causing Pea and Dot to stumble into the back of her.

"What is it?" Dot asked, a sharp look of concern on her face.

"I've just realised that we might have a starting point on what happened yesterday. Anyone who went to talk to Ethel about the lightning tree damage."

Before they could discuss this further, there was

a tinkle of a bell up ahead as the door of the post office opened, and a man stepped out with a furrowed brow and a paper tucked under his arm. He wore a thick, grey, woollen jumper and dark chinos. The item of clothing that really stood out, though, was the dog collar.

"It's the vicar," Mary said quietly. "We need to talk to him. You two wait here a minute."

She left the others standing, still in a state of confusion, and marched towards the figure who had now noticed them and was forcing a smile with difficulty.

"Oh, hello," he said as Mary reached him.

"I'm sorry we haven't managed to meet yet," Mary said with what she hoped was a pleasant smile. "My name's Mary Blake, I'm up at Blancham Hall?" She raised her voice into a question, wondering if this new vicar had been told about the manor hidden across the fields yet.

"Oh, I know who you are!" He said, his smile becoming more genuine as his eyes widened in recognition. "Mary Blake! I'm a big fan!" He took her hand in both of his and shook it vigorously. "I've vowed never to watch *Her Law* again since they got rid of you. It is hard though!" He chuckled. "I must confess I was quite addicted before."

Mary smiled. The man's light blue eyes twinkled,

and his pleasant round face made him instantly like him. "Thank you, that's very kind." She said with a slight chuckle. "I was wondering if we could have a quick word, actually? About what's happened down at the Lightning Tree this morning?"

His face clouded instantly. "I'm afraid I've only just heard," he said, his eyes darting back towards the post office behind him. "Terrible business." He shook his head and sighed deeply. "I was just making my way over there now."

"I don't think there's anything you can do," Mary said, not wanting to head back herself. "The police have the place locked up pretty tight."

He hesitated for a moment, frowning and causing his ample, grey-flecked eyebrows to knit together. He looked up and over Mary's shoulder towards the green and saw Dot and Pea, who had been hanging back and talking amongst themselves, for the first time. His expressive face moved from concern to confusion, and then to his warm smile.

"Dot Tanner?!" He called out, laughing and moving past Mary towards her friend. "I don't believe it! It is you!"

Dot smiled, and there was something in it that surprised Mary. It was a bashful, almost shy smile that Mary wasn't sure she had ever seen on her friend. It made her look younger.

"Hello Reggie," Dot said warmly as the two embraced.

"I say!" Pea said in surprise, his eyes almost bulging from his head as they snapped between Mary and the embracing couple in alarm.

"Sorry," Dot said, shaking her head and pulling away from the vicar. "Pea? This is Reginald Downe, we went to school together."

"Oh, right," Pea said, his cheeks red. "Good to meet you." He extended his hand, and the vicar shook it warmly. "I'm Percy Blake, Mary's sister. I mean, she's my sister, I'm her brother."

Reggie chuckled as Pea reddened further. "Of course you are, a pleasure to meet you," he said before quickly turning his attention back to Dot. "So, what brings you here?"

"I'm working with Mary and Percy," Dot answered.

Reggie's eyes widened. "This new detective agency!" He said excitedly, turning to Mary. "I was quite amazed when I heard you were following in the footsteps of Susan Law!"

"Not quite," Mary smiled. "I'm hoping to have less near-death incidents than my on-screen character for one."

The vicar chuckled and shook his head. "Of course! And you are working with my old friend Dot, quite amazing. You'll all have to come to the vicarage for tea sometime." He turned back to Dot. "I'd love to catch up properly and find out how you got into all this excitement!"

"That would be lovely," Dot answered.

For a moment, the four of them stood in silence. Although Mary felt it was an uneasy one for her and Pea, she got the impression that Dot and Reggie Downe were lost in memories of the past.

"Did you know Ethel Long well?" She said, breaking the silence.

The vicar's gaze jerked away from Dot with a look of surprise. "I've only been here a few months, but I've made a point of getting to know everyone. Ethel was an important member of this community. She'll leave a big hole in the village."

Mary nodded, intrigued by his choice of words.

"I really must be going, I feel I should be with my parishioners." He turned back to Dot. "Please, call in on me at the vicarage while you're here, tomorrow maybe?"

"Definitely," Dot answered, smiling.

He placed his hands on her arms and gazed at her again. "It really is fantastic to see you, you know."

"You too," she answered.

There was another pause until the vicar shook himself from his thoughts and turned to Mary and

Pea. "Such a pleasure to meet you both." He smiled before heading off towards the village green. Dot turned to watch him go.

"Old school friend, eh?" Pea said in a voice that Mary was sure was supposed to be lighthearted, but hadn't entirely pulled it off.

"What?" Dot said, turning back towards them as though she had been wrenched from a dream. "Oh, yes, an old school friend." She cleared her throat and brushed some imaginary dust from her dark blue woollen coat. "Shall we go and talk to the people who run the shop?" She said suddenly, heading off in that direction. Mary watched her pass, noticing her reddened cheeks. Pea followed with a concerned expression and Mary fell in behind them.

CHAPTER EIGHT

The small brass bell positioned above the door chimed as they entered the cluttered shop, its stacked shelves covered in a dull yellow light from the strip lights above. The counter to their left was un-manned, and the rest of the small shop appeared to be empty.

"They must be out the back," Pea said and raising his voice, called out. "Hello?"

"Coming!" A voice called back through the open arch at the back of the shop. It was soon followed by Charles Cotton, his small, round figure emerging through the opening with his customary waddle.

"Oh, hello," he said, pausing as he saw them and looking nervously back over his shoulder. "What can I get you?" He moved behind the counter and looked up at the three of them expectantly.

"Actually," Mary said, taking the lead, "we just wanted to check you were ok after this morning? It must have been a shock finding the body like that?"

Charles blinked in silence for a moment, his eyes flicking towards the back room again. "Yes, it was rather. I'm fine though, thank you." He leaned across the counter, his head now jerking between the door to the backroom and Mary. "You won't tell them Gloria went to see Ethel yesterday, will you? No need to mention that and add to the confusion." Mary stared at him in surprise, unsure what to say. "I mean," he continued, "they might think it looks a bit funny, what with me finding her and everything." He swallowed as he stood back up and gave them all a nervous smile.

"Tell me everything about how you found her," Mary said in an even tone. "What position was she in? What was she wearing? What were these symbols like that were drawn on her?"

Charles visibly shuddered as Mary's quickfire questions hit him.

"Oh god," he mumbled quietly. "It was so horrible."

"Quick, Charles, before whoever is through the back, that you don't want to hear this comes out."

He looked at the doorway again and then began speaking in a low, rapid voice. "It was Bessy, my dog, she was barking and growling and all sorts as we got to the green. We normally make a loop of the village first thing, she needs the toilet quite a bit now as she gets older, so I have to get up early to..."

"Just cut to when you found her," Mary said, not wanting to hear about Bessy's bladder control.

"I didn't even see her at first," he said, his eyes now focused on something none of them could see, on the memory of that morning. "It was still quite dark, and you know how deep the opening in the tree is."

"She was actually inside the opening?"

He nodded and swallowed again. "She was laying back in it like she was on a sun lounger, she would have almost looked peaceful if it wasn't for... Oh god." He shook his head.

"What is it?"

"She had blood on her hair, on her face, and her eyes were staring at me! Oh, it was horrible!"

"What was she wearing?"

He frowned, as though the question had snapped him out of the memory and confused him. "Wearing? Just her normal clothes, some blue dress, and a cardigan, but those symbols."

"What were they like?" Pea asked.

"They were very occult," Charles said

meaningfully. "They looked like some sort of witchcraft to me."

"Seen a lot of witchcraft, have you?" Dot asked.

"Well, no," Charles admitted, before suddenly looking up as voices came from the door to the backroom.

"I really don't want you to go to any trouble," a man's voice said.

"Oh, don't be silly, it's no problem at all!" Replied Gloria Cotton, who emerged through the doorway followed by a police officer. She stopped as she saw the small crowd that was gathered in the little shop. "Oh, hello Mary, Percy." She gave a weak smile at each of them before nodding slightly towards Dot and turning to the officer next to her. "Charles, I was just going to make Constable Porter here a bit of early lunch. The poor lad has been up since the crack of dawn."

The young man's cheeks reddened. "There's no need, just a cup of tea would be fine."

"Nonsense," Gloria said. "Will you be wanting something, Charles?"

"Um, yes, thank you."

"Is everything ok here?" the officer said, looking at the group. His sheepish grin slid from his face and was replaced by a keen, professional look.

"I was just getting some stamps," Mary answered

quickly. "Shocking news this morning, do the police have any idea what happened yet?"

The officer paused a moment and then smiled. "I'm not allowed to talk about the case I'm afraid."

"Of course not." Mary beamed back before turning to Gloria. "How are you, Gloria?"

"Oh, fine, fine. All a bit of a shock all this." She smiled, but it didn't seem to reach her eyes. If Mary didn't know better, she would have sworn that she looked scared.

"Here are your stamps," Charles said, placing a book of six on the counter.

Mary turned to him frowning, before realising she had in fact just asked for them. "Right, yes." She fished in her pocket for change as Gloria headed back through the doorway with the officer in tow.

"Why did Gloria go to see Ethel yesterday?" Mary asked in a low voice once they had gone.

"She didn't see her in the end," he replied. "You know that: you were there."

"That's not what she asked," Dot said. "Why did she go and see her at all?"

"I don't see why that's any of your business," Charles snapped. "I don't even know who you are!"

"Her name is Dot, and she works with Mary and me," Pea said in a loud, defensive voice.

"Ok, ok!" Charles said, his eyes darting to the

back doorway again. "There's no need for raised voices."

"What is it you're so nervous about?" Mary asked, folding her arms and fixing him with a stare.

"What do you expect?!" Charles hissed. "I found somebody murdered this morning! The police are at my house!"

"Is everything ok out here?" The young officer appeared in the doorway, his face etched in concern.

"All fine!" Mary smiled. "Emotions just running a bit high with everything that's happened."

The Constable studied them all for a moment before nodding. "Of course." He remained in the doorway, apparently not entirely convinced by Mary's explanation.

"We better be going," Mary said brightly. "We'll see you soon, Charles."

"Yes, right," the shopkeeper answered gruffly.

Mary, Dot, and Pea left with the small bell ringing out again above them.

"That was all a bit odd," Pea said, exhaling in the cold air.

"They were both very jumpy," Dot agreed, "But I guess that's to be expected after finding a body."

"Gloria, though?" Mary said. "She didn't find the body, and for all her cheeriness, she looked just as worried as Charles to me."

"Really?" Pea said in surprise. "I thought she was on pretty good form. Awfully nice of her to offer that officer a spot of lunch, I almost asked if I could get in on the act. I'm starving."

Mary shook her head. "She was playing the role well, but I saw her eyes. They were both worried about something, and it wasn't just the discovery of the body." She took a deep breath and looked back down the road towards the direction of the village green. "Actually, maybe a spot of lunch at the Cauldron wouldn't be a bad idea."

Dot nodded shrewdly, guessing that Mary wanted to make sure they missed none of the village gossip. Pea merely beamed.

"Excellent idea!" He said and strode off ahead.

CHAPTER NINE

The tables outside the Cauldron had gone when they had arrived. So had most of the police presence. Just two uniformed officers were left by the still erect crime scene tent, sheltering under the boughs of the tree from the light drizzle that had begun to fall.

As they stepped inside the warm interior of the Cauldron, all eyes in the room turned to them. There was the briefest of pauses in the general murmur of conversation before, having recognised them as locals, it returned.

"Have you heard?" Frank said as they approached the bar.

"Heard what?" Pea asked.

Frank looked along the bar where a few locals

were gathered at the far end before leaning forward and talking in a low voice.

"Robert Woods has been arrested!"

Mary and Pea both looked at each other open-mouthed.

"Who's Robert Woods?" Dot asked.

"Ah, of course," Frank said. "You won't know him, not being from around here. He's our local odd-job man, lives out at Elm Cottage."

"Blimey, that was quick work! But why have they arrested him?" Pea asked. "Have they found some sort of evidence?"

"I don't know the ins and outs of it," admitted Frank reluctantly, "but everyone knows what he's like."

"I don't," Dot said.

"He's a trouble maker," Frank added.

"That's a bit harsh, isn't it?" Pea said. "He's a young lad who's had a rough deal. Bound to get in a spot of bother now and then."

"Yeah, well," Frank said nodding. "Can't say it wasn't sad what happened to his parents, but maybe that's what sent him over the edge to kill poor old Ethel?"

"I think you're probably jumping the gun a bit there Frank, are you sure he's been arrested?" Mary said.

"They took him off in their car," Frank said defensively.

"Why don't we wait and see what they wanted to talk to him about? In the meantime, we were hoping we could get some lunch?"

"Ah sorry, can't help you there. Still haven't found a new cook yet and Alice has gone off chasing Robert to the police station in a taxi, so it's just me."

"Of course!" Pea said. "Alice and Robert are a bit of an item, aren't they?"

"Against my better judgement," Frank muttered. He looked up along the bar and waved a hand at a large jar where eggs bobbed ominously in a murky liquid sea of vinegar. "We've got pickled eggs?"

"No thanks," Mary said hurriedly, hoping he didn't notice her involuntarily shudder at the thought. "We should probably be getting on anyway. Speak to you later."

She gestured to the others, and the three of them left, exiting the gloom of the pub and heading back into the dull grey outside. Mary was already pulling the phone from her pocket before anyone else could speak. Dot took note and pulled Pea away from her by the arm so that they made a different route around the village green, the Lightning Tree, and the murder scene.

The phone rang out in Mary's ear, and she hung

up without leaving a message and called straight back again. This time though, Inspector Joe Corrigan answered on the ninth ring.

"You know I'm busy right now?" he said upon answering.

"And you know that's why I'm calling," Mary countered. "Rumour is you've arrested someone already?"

"You shouldn't believe rumours."

"Unfortunately, that's all I have to go on as the police don't seem to be sharing any details with me."

"Mary," Corrigan said sighing. "You know I can't give you every detail of an active case. You're lucky that I tell you anything."

"You haven't!" Mary protested, prompting another sigh.

"We haven't arrested anyone, we've just brought someone in to answer a few questions."

"Robert Woods."

There was a slight pause before Corrigan answered, "News really does travel fast there, doesn't it?"

"What questions have you got for him?"

"I need to go, Mary, but you can ask him yourself later, he'll be heading back to the village soon enough."

The line went dead, causing Mary to swear as

she met Dot and Pea on the far side of the triangular village green from the pub.

"What's the news?" Pea asked expectantly.

"Nothing useful, but Robert Woods hasn't been arrested, they're releasing him soon." She trailed off as an idea came to mind. "Pea, young Alice at the pub doesn't drive, does she? Frank said she'd got a taxi to the police station?"

"That's right."

"And Robert was driven there in a police car, so why don't we offer them a lift back to the village?"

Pea grinned at her. "Good thinking!"

"And how is your policeman going to feel about that?" Dot asked with one raised eyebrow.

"He's not my policeman, and I couldn't care less what he thinks," Mary answered, realising that she sounded like a schoolgirl denying a crush.

CHAPTER TEN

M ary stood up as the door at the back of the small reception room opened, and Robert Woods and Alice Crowther passed into the room hand in hand.

"Oh, hello Mary," Alice said, a look of surprise passing across her pretty, round face. She looked tired and pale, but a smile still appeared on her lips. She had come to the village two years ago, answering an advert for a job at the pub. Anything to get her away from the abusive family she had left in Tanbury. Frank had taken a liking to her and had let her rent a room from him at The Cauldron. With no family of his own, Pea had told Mary that Frank had taken to her like a daughter.

"Are you ok?" Mary said, moving towards both of them and placing a hand on Alice's arm.

"Yes, thank you," Robert answered.

He was a striking-looking young man, with dark hair and eyes to match. His cheekbones were so sharp they looked as though they could cut you, and he had a tragic past. Both his parents had been killed in a car accident four years ago when he was just 18.

Corrigan appeared through the door behind them and shook his head slightly as he saw Mary.

"We've come to give you a lift back to the village," Mary said to the young couple. "Pea's out in the car, I'll be out in a minute."

Robert looked suspicious, but Alice merely nodded and pulled her boyfriend towards the door.

"Very charitable of you," Corrigan said once they had gone.

"I like to do my bit for my local community," Mary answered, staring him down.

He sighed and shook his head again. "Ok, you win. We brought him in because he was seen arguing with the victim the day before she was killed."

"Arguing with her? About what?"

"That's what I'd like to know. The lad isn't saying anything to us. Says he was just calling in on her to see if she wanted any odd jobs doing around the place."

"Who's the witness?"

Corrigan's eyebrow raised, and one corner of his

mouth rose slightly. "Maybe I'll tell you their name if you can tell me what that young man and the victim were arguing about?"

"And what makes you think he'll tell me?"

"Oh, come on Mary. You're a glamorous woman and a celebrity. He's more likely to open up to you than us lot here. Just try."

"I'll let you know," Mary said, turning to the door.

"Mary," he called after. She turned back to him, one hand on the door. "It's good to see you."

She ignored the fluttering in her stomach and lifted her chin in the air. "I should hope so," she answered cooly, before turning and walking out of the station.

She could see Alice Crowther's pale face at the back window of the car, staring out at the front of the police station. Her eyes were unseeing until Mary was just a few feet from the car when they suddenly focused, and she smiled.

Pea had driven, as usual, and Dot had remained at the manor. Robert and Alice were in the back seat together, and so Mary slid into the passenger seat.

"How are you both doing?" She said as Pea eased them away from the curb and into the street and she turned back towards them. "It must have been quite a shock?"

"You can say that again," Alice said, taking a deep breath.

"It's just all so stupid," Robert added angrily. "I never touched Ethel."

"And if that's the case, you've got nothing to worry about," Mary said.

"It is," Robert said firmly.

"Ok then," Mary nodded. "Did they tell you why they wanted to speak to you?"

Alice was sat on the opposite side of the car to Mary, and she saw her look at Robert anxiously. "They wanted to know where I was last night. I told them I was working in the pub until late and then went up to my room to read."

"And what about you, Robert?" Mary asked, twisting further to look at him. He was looking out of the window now. His eyes glazed over, and a deep frown on his forehead.

"Robert?" Alice said, her voice full of concern.

He turned as though just hearing them for the first time. "Sorry, what?"

"What were they asking you?" Alice said, repeating Mary's question.

He looked from her to Mary.

"It's ok," Mary said. "You can trust us."

"This is such a nightmare," he said, rubbing his hands through his hair.

"Maybe we can help you?" Mary said softly. "Tell us what's going on."

Robert took a deep breath as Alice took his right hand in hers. "I went to see Ethel yesterday, they say someone saw me arguing with her."

"Arguing with her?" Alice said, clearly shocked. "What about?"

He looked at her and then at Mary as though deciding something.

"It's ok Robert," Mary said, "we're on your side here."

He nodded and took a deep breath. "I've had letters."

Alice frowned. "What kind of letters?"

"Nasty ones," Robert answered bitterly. "About my parents. Saying that maybe I had something to do with their accident. I was the one who got everything after they died, so they think I killed them."

"Oh my god, that's horrible!" Alice exclaimed, her hands taking both of Robert's. "Why didn't you tell me?"

"I don't know." He shrugged. "I didn't want you to think there might be some truth in it, I guess."

"You idiot," Alice said, punching him playfully on the arm. "Of course I wouldn't have!"

He smiled at her. "Thanks."

"But why would that have made you argue with

Ethel?" Mary asked from the front. "Did you think she might be sending them?"

Robert looked sharply up at her. "Yes, I did. Everyone knows what she's like. Always sticking her nose in other people's business."

"I can remember her making you a fair amount of meals after your parents died," Mary said.

"Probably only to try and get more gossip on how I was feeling, or what was happening to the house."

Mary felt somehow that is heart wasn't in this last comment. He had looked down, as though now doubting the version of events he was describing.

"It could have been anyone," Mary continued. "Everyone knew what had happened. Maybe someone just wanted to get at you for some reason? Can you think of anyone who might have a grudge against you that might want to do that?"

"No, not really. I mean, I've been in the odd fight in Adderbury after I've had a few, but none of them knew anything about my parents."

"And what were you doing last night?"

His eyes seem to flare with anger. "So you think I did it as well then?"

"No, but I know the police would have asked you, so I need to as well if I'm going to help you."

"I was at home, on my own."

Mary nodded and turned back to the front. Pea

shot her a glance but remained silent. Presumably knowing that Mary was making headway and it was best not to rock the boat.

"Did you tell the police about these letters you received?" She called over her shoulder.

"No, I didn't want to give them any more reasons for them to think I did it."

"And do you still have these letters?"

"No, I threw them away."

Mary cursed in her head. She wasn't sure if the letters were anything to do with Ethel's murder, but it all seemed quite a coincidence. Poison pen letters, a threatening message written onto the Lightning Tree, Ethel's death, and the symbols that were found on her clothing.

Something strange and sinister was happening in Bloxley, and she was determined to get to the bottom of it.

She looked up and saw they had reached the village green. The crime scene tent was gone now, and she knew there would be nothing there to look at. She needed to know more about Ethel, she needed to find out why someone would have taken the brutal step of murdering her, and where the Lightning Tree and its horrible past might fit in.

CHAPTER ELEVEN

M ary woke early and was downstairs, munching on a piece of toast when Dot entered.

"Morning," her old friend said as she took a seat next to her at the snooker table that had become their desk. "What's the plan for today?"

"I've been thinking about the letters Robert said he'd got," Mary answered, too lost in thought for niceties. "I'm wondering if other people in the village have had letters as well."

"Why would you think that?"

Mary finished the last of her toast and washed it down with a swig of coffee before continuing. "There's something strange about the letters. I couldn't put my finger on it yesterday, but now I've got it. They aren't specific at all."

Dot's brow furrowed. "What do you mean?"

"Why go to the effort of writing letters like that to someone, when you don't really have anything to say? It's not like whoever wrote them had some sort of evidence that Robert had done something to cause his parents' accident. They were just making vague assumptions because he got the money."

"Ok, but I still don't see why that would mean other people had had letters as he did?"

"What has everyone been saying about the atmosphere in the village recently? Hetty said everyone's been on edge, there have been arguments in the pub, in the shop."

"Are you saying that the whole village might have been receiving these?!" Dot said in alarm. "Who on earth would do that?"

"I don't know, but I thought a good start would be to take your old school friend up on his offer of tea at the vicarage. I'd like to ask him why he was arguing with George Copeland in the Cauldron last week."

"You can't think Reggie had anything to do with it?!" Dot said, clearly outraged at the idea.

"Just because you know him at school, doesn't mean we should keep him on the suspect list," Pea said as he came through the door, having heard the end of the conversation from the hallway.

"Exactly," Mary added as Dot folded her arms,

scowling. "Then I think we should work through the names of the people who were in the pub the night the tree was vandalised." She held up the piece of paper that Frank Roach had written out for her two days ago.

"Sounds good to me," Pea said. "Maybe you'd want to stay out of us talking to the vicar Dot?" He added hopefully. "I don't want you to feel awkward."

"The only thing that's going to make me feel awkward is you being stupid enough to think Reggie could be involved," she replied haughtily, before rising from her chair and heading back towards the hallway. "It's a nice day, I think I'll walk into the village if anyone wants to join me?"

Mary and Pea exchanged glances, hers was one of amusement until she saw the concern in his and quickly adopted a more suitable look.

"Come on then," she said, putting her arm on Pea's back and guiding him towards the door. "It looks like we're going for a walk."

They headed into the hallway where Dot was already in her coat and wrapping a scarf tightly around her neck, when there was a knock on the large rounded front door. Pea opened it to reveal the vicar with a worried expression, his hair tousled from the stiff breeze.

"Oh, hello vicar," Pea said, in a tone that Mary

thought was a little obvious in terms of disappointment, though the vicar didn't seem to notice.

"Morning. Sorry to come by unannounced, but I just haven't been able to get the horrible incident yesterday out of my mind. I was wondering if you would be kind enough to offer me some advice?" His eyes had peered past Pea and locked onto Dot's, which he suddenly seemed to become aware of as he then looked at Mary and Pea. "From all of you, I mean."

"Of course vicar, please, come in."

He smiled and looked up at Pea who still half blocked the doorway with a frown.

"Pea?" Mary said, making him snap out of his thoughts with a jolt.

"Oh, right. Yes, come in," he said, moving aside so the vicar could enter the hall.

"Let me take your coat," Dot said, moving towards him. "And would you like some tea?"

"That would be lovely," he answered, smiling.

"Why don't you go and make some for all of us?" Dot said to Pea as she guided the vicar into the billiard room office.

His mouth opened and closed again noiselessly.

"Oh, go on," Mary said, rolling her eyes at him

and slapping him on the arm as she followed the others.

"So do you have some thoughts on who might have committed the murder?" Dot asked as she gestured for the vicar to take a seat.

"Oh! No, nothing like that," he answered nervously. "In fact, that's sort of the problem really."

"In what way?" Mary asked, standing on the opposite side of the snooker table from where Dot and the vicar had taken seats.

The vicar cleared his throat before beginning. "Of course, you'll know that I can't in all good consciousness give away any confidences of my parishioners."

"I think that might depend on whether that information could bring a killer to justice, don't you?" Mary said, causing Dot to shoot her a sharp look.

"I'm sure it has no bearing on finding the murderer," he answered, his head shaking. "But I must admit I think it does seem like something the police should be aware of."

"Ok then, let's hear it."

He took a deep breath and opened his mouth to speak when Pea returned with a pot of tea and cups on a tray.

"Have I missed anything yet?" he asked as he set the tray down on the snooker table.

"The vicar was just about to tell us what is worrying him," Mary replied.

"Yes," the vicar continued as Dot did the honours and poured tea for them all. "Someone from the village came to me around two weeks ago in some distress. They had received a rather nasty letter."

"A letter?" Mary asked, exchanging glances with the others.

"Yes, a letter which was quite threatening."

"Did you see it?"

"No, I didn't, I'm afraid." The vicar paused for a moment. "I have to say you don't sound shocked by this?"

"That's because we've heard of someone else receiving a letter like this," Dot said.

Mary glanced at her, unsure at how much information they should be sharing, but then realised the vicar could well be talking about Robert Woods.

"My goodness," the vicar said, "who was it?"

"Robert Woods," Dot answered.

"Oh!" The vicar reeled back in shock. "Poor Robert, after all he's been through in life!"

"You know of his parents' accident then?" Pea asked.

"Oh, yes, so tragic. I had no idea he had been the victim of this awfulness though, it wasn't him I had been speaking of."

"Do you at least know what the letter this other person said?" Mary continued.

"Not exactly, but it sounded as though it was all rather vague threats I'm afraid, but..." he looked around the three of them as he ran his tongue across his dry lips.

"What is it?" Mary pressed. "If there's something, anything you know that you think could be of use, you need to tell us. We can tell you if it's worthy of the police."

He nodded. "Yes, yes, that is why I came after all. I just don't like getting involved in gossip." He sighed and straightened himself in his chair. "This person speculated about who they thought might have sent the letter, but never explicitly said, however." He looked up at Dot, his face full of concern. "It is only my impression, but from things they said, I rather think they suspected Ethel Long."

Mary and Pea exchanged glances, but Dot's remained fixed on the vicar.

"And you suspect this person, therefore, might well have had a reason to bump the old girl off," Pea said in amazement.

"Oh no, I'm sure..." He seemed to catch himself before continuing. "I'm sure this person wouldn't dream of such a thing."

"Do you know why they thought it might be Ethel?" Mary asked.

"I've no idea. As you know, I haven't been in the village very long, but I understand she had a reputation for..." He trailed off again.

Dot jumped in to finish the sentence. "She was a gossip from what I've heard."

"Quite," he smiled, "but she'd always been very polite and welcoming to me."

"I'm sorry, vicar," Mary said, "But you really are going to have to tell the police and give up the name of the person who told you this."

He frowned, closed his eyes, and pinched the bridge of his nose. "Do you really think that is necessary? I'm quite sure this person had nothing to do with poor Mrs Long's death."

"That's not for you to decide though is it, old boy?" Pea said. "You can't go around being judge and jury when someone's died."

The vicar looked up at him in shock. "Oh, I would never...yes, yes you're right." He stood up and ran his hand over his brow. I will talk to the police, but I think it only right to speak to the person who gave me their confidence beforehand. They may like to accompany me to talk to the police."

"Or," Dot answered, "if they are the murderer, they could decide to keep you quiet permanently."

"Oh my! Surely not!" The vicar's voice rose in panic.

"She's right," Mary chimed in, "If this person is the killer, you could be in serious danger."

"But surely..." The man's eyes darted around the floor, his forehead furrowed in thought. "I'm afraid I will need to think this over," he said, at last, looking up at Dot. "I hope you understand that this is a matter of conscience for me?"

"Of course," Dot replied. "You want to do the right thing, we can understand that."

"Blowed if I can," Pea exclaimed. "Chap could be letting a bloody murderer roam loose in the village!"

"I think Reggie is perfectly capable of judging the situation on his own," Dot countered with a tone that had spikes in.

"I'm not sure he is," Pea answered, pulling himself upright and folding his arms, "blighter's going to get himself, or someone else, killed."

"I can assure you, I will not let that happen!" The vicar said firmly, pulling himself upright. "I think it best if I go now." He turned to Dot and took her hand. "I'm sorry, Dorothy, but we will have to postpone our catchup."

"Of course," Dot said, "but please be careful won't you?"

He smiled at her, turned it towards Mary for a moment before heading towards the door with a curt nod at Pea as he passed.

They said nothing until the sound of the front door closing caused Pea to break the silence.

"I'm going to follow him," Pea said.

"I beg your pardon?!" Dot exclaimed.

"I'm going to follow him," Pea repeated. "If he's going to talk to the murderer, then all I have to do is follow him and see who it is."

"You don't know he's going to talk to the murderer!" Dot snapped. "We now know of two people who got these nasty letters, it could be that half the village got them!"

"Still," Pea countered, "If he doesn't tell us who this person is, I'm going to jolly well find out."

"And betray his confidence?"

"I'm not in his confidence! I've only just met the blighter!"

Dot's eyes hardened into two small dark and dangerous points.

"I think I'm going to go for that walk, but on my own," she said firmly, before rising and leaving the room.

Pea moved to the window as Mary cursed inwardly as she realised she hadn't even asked the vicar about the altercation in the pub with George Copeland.

"Unless you really are going to follow the vicar," Mary said, joining her brother at the window, "I think you should come with me to talk to George Copeland and find out why he was arguing with the vicar last week."

"I can't imagine anyone not arguing with that man," Pea muttered, "Besides, there's no chance of following him right now." He gestured out of the window. In the distance, the figure of the vicar had stopped and turned, with Dot hurrying towards him.

CHAPTER TWELVE

The fact that Bloxley had a butcher at all was always quite a surprise to visitors. Although it was true that the village itself was hardly big enough to sustain it, the ten or so surrounding communities all travelled to Bloxley for their meat rather than making the longer, more time-consuming trip to Tanbury.

On the short drive into the village, Mary had pretended not to see Pea craning his neck in the driver's seat in an attempt to catch a glimpse of Dot and the vicar. The path, though, had already wound its way into the woods and there was no sign of them.

Now, as they pulled up outside Copeland's Butchers, his face had set into a grim, shut-down expression.

"Shall we pick up some nice steaks for dinner

tonight?" Mary asked as they climbed out of the vehicle.

Pea's face brightened slightly.

"Oh, yes, good idea," he nodded.

Mary smiled to herself as she entered the shop. Pea was always easily cheered up via the stomach.

"Morning, Mary!" George said as she entered. "Haven't seen you for a while, but I hear you're back at the hall?"

"That's right George, how are things?"

"Oh you know, can't complain."

Going against the usual image of a rotund and rosy-cheeked butcher, George Copeland was a thin figure with elongated features that gave him an almost hound dog look.

"We were just after a few steaks if you have anything good in?" Pea asked.

Mary couldn't decide whether he was getting better at being discreet when finding out information, or if he really had become so focused on the steaks that he'd forgotten their real purpose. Her money was on the latter.

"Oh, you've come at the right time!" George answered, rubbing his hands together in glee. "Got a few top sirloins in that you're going to love!"

Mary watched as George proudly displayed a specimen to Pea who seemed suitably impressed to the point where she thought his mouth was actually watering.

"Can you believe what's happened to poor old Ethel Long?" George said as he began to wrap the steaks. "It's not doing Beryl's blood pressure any good, that's for sure."

"So awful," Mary agreed, glad that he had broached the subject himself before she had to. "I just can't think why anyone would do it."

George's hands paused, momentarily above the packaging.

"Well, you know what Ethel was like," he said slowly as he resumed the wrapping. "She was one for getting involved in other people's business."

There was something in his tone that made Mary and Pea exchange glances. Conscious that he had almost finished wrapping the last steak, Mary decided to get to the point of their visit.

"I heard you had a bit of excitement in the pub yourself last week, George?"

He looked up at her sharply as he placed the wrapped steaks into a large paper bag.

"You had a bit of a row with the vicar?"

George frowned. "That was just a little misunderstanding, nothing to do with the vicar. All a fuss about nothing."

"What was it about then?"

George's eyes narrowed slightly. "Do you know, I can't even remember now. Silly how things happen, isn't it?" He smiled as he tapped at the till and Pea handed over the cash for the steaks.

"Thanks for these," Pea said, looking at the bag he held as though it held the Crown Jewels.

"One more thing," Mary added as they moved towards the door. "You haven't had any nasty letters, have you?"

George's smile flickered at the edges, his eyes widening slightly.

"What do you mean, nasty letters?"

"It seems there's been a bit of a spate of them in the village, I was just wondering if you'd had one?"

Something passed across the man's long face, but Mary wasn't sure what.

"Is this to do with Ethel's death?" He said, throwing Mary slightly. She glanced at Pea, who was hovering in the doorway.

"Why would you say that?"

The butcher blinked back at her for a moment before making a dismissive gesture with his right hand. "Oh, I don't know, you were just asking about both that's all. I've not had any letters or anything no."

"Right," Mary said, holding his gaze for a moment. "We'll get off then. See you around."

"Bye," he smiled at them both as they left the shop and headed out onto the street.

"What do you think?" Pea said as they reached the car.

"I think he was nervous about something," Mary answered.

"Everyone in the village seems to be nervous about something or other," Pea muttered as he got in the car. He held the paper bag out to her as she climbed into the passenger seat. "Here, hold these, will you?"

Mary turned and tossed the bag onto the back seat.

"Hey! Be careful with those!" Pea cried, his face contorted in concern.

"Oh, for goodness sake!" Mary said, eyes rolling, "Let's just get going, shall we?"

"Home?" Pea asked as he fired up the car. His tone suggesting he was still worried about the steaks but was willing to let it go for now.

"No, I think we should go to Tanbury hospital and check in on Mrs Parchment."

"What do you want to see her for?"

"She was close to Ethel, maybe she knows of a reason someone might want to have hurt her."

"Ok, but we're popping home first and getting these steaks in the fridge," Pea said firmly.

"Fine," Mary sighed before sitting upright as she spotted a familiar figure making its way down the pavement. "Oh, it's Dot. Pull over and see if she wants to come."

Pea guided the car across to the pavement and lowered his window.

"Hi," he said with a sheepish grin. "We've bought some lovely steaks for dinner tonight."

"Fine," Dot answered in a flat tone.

"We're heading to the hospital to see one of Ethel's friends. We thought she might know something," Mary said, leaning across her brother.

"Ok," Dot answered, before climbing in the back seat.

Pea pulled away with Mary watching his pale, nervous face, eyes glancing at his rearview mirror with concern.

CHAPTER THIRTEEN

D orothy Parchment was on a small ward in Tanbury General hospital, containing only three other beds. Two were unoccupied, and the third contained an elderly woman who was snoring softly when Mary and Dot entered. Pea, having been sent off to rustle up some tea and biscuits. Dorothy herself was in the bed closest to the door and was sat up, reading a newspaper.

"Hi Mrs Parchment," Mary said quietly, hoping not to wake the sleeping woman in the next bed.

"Mary! What a lovely surprise!" She beamed, turning to them and placing the newspaper at her side.

Her eyes were ringed with dark lines, her cheeks pale.

"This is my friend Dot," Mary said, gesturing to

her as she took one of the two blue plastic chairs that stood nearby and Dot the other.

"Nice to meet you," Mrs Parchment said, sitting up slightly straighter, "Sorry I look such a mess."

"No one can look at their best in hospital," Dot smiled back.

"How are you?" Mary asked.

"Oh, you know, getting there," she sighed, "But this business with Ethel, I just can't believe it!" Her eyes shone with emotion. Mary wondered if the dark lines were related to her recovery from hip surgery, or if it was due to tears over her friend's death.

Mrs Parchment lifted the paper she had just discarded and waved it. "And have you seen this? Disgusting it is! Poor Ethel, having the whole world gawping at her like that."

Mary stared at the picture on the front page. The lighting tree stood, etched in black and white, at its base a figure. The face was blurred out, but the dark dress that covered the body was clear enough to make out several symbols drawn across it in a dull white. They were hard to see, but Mary could just about make out moons and pentagrams amongst the other squiggles.

"Blimey," Mary said breathlessly. "I can't believe they printed that."

"I know!" She agreed.

"Someone must want it to be picked up by the nationals for a payday," Dot said. Mrs Parchment put the paper down and reached for a tissue from a box on the table next to her. She blew her nose loudly.

"I'm so sorry," Mary said, reaching out and taking her hand. "I know the two of you were close."

Mrs Parchment gave a small laugh. "Well, as close as anyone could be to Ethel, she was a funny old bird."

"She was," Mary smiled back. "We were looking into why someone had defaced the lightning tree, but now we're wondering if they were connected, bearing in mind where Ethel was found. Can you think of anyone who might have had a grudge against her?"

Mrs Parchment looked at her with a sudden, fierce intensity. "That bloody tree," she said, shaking her head. "Ethel caused quite a fuss when she wrote that little book saying it was nothing to do with witchcraft."

"You don't think that could have driven someone to murder, do you?"

"Who knows?" she answered. "I know Frank Roach was furious about it all, said she was trying to put him out of business."

"And was she?" Dot asked.

Mrs Parchment looked at her in surprise, but then her raised eyebrows dropped as she smiled.

"I don't think she was trying to put him out of business, but she certainly liked to ruffle feathers." The smile faded slightly. "Of course, then there was this recent trouble."

"Recent trouble?" Mary prompted.

"A few weeks ago, Ethel said that she thought someone was playing games in the village."

"What sort of games?"

"She said someone was spreading spiteful letters saying all sorts of nasty things."

"How did she know this? Did she get one?"

"Do you know," Flo said thoughtfully, "she was rather cagey about that. I asked her of course, but Ethel only ever gave away what she wanted to."

"Then how did she know about them?" Dot asked.

The elderly woman leaned forward and spoke in a low voice. "Someone confronted her about them!"

"What do you mean confronted her?"

"Well, they thought she'd sent it! Ridiculous! Ethel liked to have a bit of a gossip and tease people a little, but she was a good woman at heart. She'd never do anything deliberately nasty. Believe me, the way everyone in the village always tells her everything." She shook her head and laughed. "She had enough secrets that she could have written these letters years ago if she wanted!"

"And did she tell you who it was that confronted her?" Mary asked, wanting to confirm what Robert Wood's had told her yesterday.

"No, she wouldn't, even though I asked her outright." She frowned. "Funny, though."

"What was?" Dot asked.

"Normally she would have enjoyed something like that. You know, someone getting all in a state about nothing, but she seemed different about this. She seemed I don't know, concerned almost."

"For her own safety?"

"No," Mrs Parchment said, shaking her head. "I think it was for the person she was talking about."

Mary was about to mention Robert Woods' admission that he had confronted Ethel over the letters. Before she could, they were interrupted by a familiar voice, entering the ward behind them.

"I'm sorry!" Pea said. "I got the tea and biscuits, but bumped into these two as well." He gestured backwards with his head at Inspector Joe Corrigan. The latter was being followed by a uniformed officer.

"Hello Mary, Dot," Corrigan said, nodding at them both. "It seems you got here before us. I hope you've been encouraging Mrs Parchment to be as open with us as she almost certainly has been with you?"

"Of course Inspector," Mary said curtly, rising from her chair. "We were just about to leave in any case." She turned to Mrs Parchment and gave her hand another squeeze. "I'll try and call in on you again."

"Thanks, dear, but don't you worry about me. I'm on the mend, and I'll be out of here soon enough."

"There's me, going all over the bloody hospital to find a tea machine and biscuits," Pea muttered as he placed the four cups and the pack of digestives he's brought next to the patient. "I guess you lot can have them now," he said to the police in the tone of a teenager who'd just been told they couldn't go to a house party.

"Thank you very much," Corrigan smiled as he took a tea. "I'll return the favour sometime."

Mary, Dot, and Pea made their way back out into the corridor. Mary glanced back just once as she reached the door to find Corrigan's eyes still locked on her. She turned and left without saying anything.

CHAPTER FOURTEEN

The Tanbury Gazette's offices were nestled in one corner of the main town square. The sign that declared the presence of the second-largest paper in the county of Addervale wasn't a grand or impressive one. It's faded blue background, and spotty orange lettering suggested the newspaper had seen better days, which Mary was sure was the case.

She had remembered the paper from her childhood as being something of importance. A publication that everyone in the north of the county relied upon for news and information from what, back then, was their world.

The people of North Adderbury had had their world expanded to the whole globe since then. With their information and news, now in their pockets and at their fingertips.

The sense of a place that had fallen on harder times continued inside. Mary opened the door and stepped onto a carpet worn so thin over the years that you could almost see the concrete underneath. Six desks were in the room, three against each wall, with a central path down the middle of them. All of them were empty apart from the front left, where a young woman Mary judged to be in her early twenties was seated behind a large computer screen. She hadn't even looked up as Mary had entered.

"Hello," Mary said, heading towards the woman's desk.

"Oh!" the woman squeaked, looking up in shock. "Sorry, I was miles away!"

Her eyes came to rest on Mary's where they widened in surprise.

"Mary Blake!" she said as she stood up suddenly, her wheeled office chair rolling away behind her. "We've been messaging you for an interview, but I never thought you'd come in! Please, take a seat!"

Mary smiled and took the seat that the woman wheeled towards her.

"I'm Amy by the way, can I get you a cup of tea or coffee?"

"I'm fine thanks," Mary answered.

Amy nodded and sat down, a bundle of emotional energy.

"So, how are you finding life being back in Addervale?" she asked.

"Actually," Mary said, leaning forward, "I was hoping to talk to you about the murder at Bloxley."

Amy's eyes lit up. "Oh! Of course!" Mary watched as the young woman attempted to reign in her excitement at getting a celebrity's opinion on a grizzly murder, to something more appropriate when talking about death.

"I mean," Amy continued, "it's so awful. That poor woman. Killed for her beliefs."

"Her beliefs?" Mary asked, starting in her chair.

"Yes, she was some sort of modern-day witch by all accounts, and surely you've seen the picture in the paper? Those symbols that were drawn all over her? Must be something to do with witchcraft and that tree." She gave an exaggerated shudder. "That tree gives me the creeps, and I haven't even seen it in real life!"

"Actually, that picture was one of the things I wanted to ask you about. Matt Sharpe, the man who took it. Does he work here?"

The girl laughed. "Matt? No, he doesn't work for anyone."

There was something in her tone that told Mary she had a crush on the young man in question.

"So he just turned up with the photo?" She asked.

"He sells us bits and pieces every so often," Amy answered airily, before leaning forward conspiratorially. "Actually, he says he's got a big story for us soon!"

"Oh? About what?"

"Something to do with this murder, not sure yet. Anyway," she said, straightening up, "it's your thoughts on it all I want to hear! Are you going to investigate? I mean, now you've set up your private eye business, you've got to, right? It's right on your doorstep! It could really put you on the map, more than you already are, I mean!"

"I'm just a concerned local resident," Mary answered warily. "Does anyone have any theories on what those symbols on Ethel's might mean?"

"Witchcraft!" Amy answered excitedly. "I've been reading up on the Lightning Tree, though I dare say you know all about it from living over that way." She leaned forward conspiratorially. "Did you know that the victim wrote a book saying that all the legends about witchcraft and magic to do with that tree were nonsense?"

"I've read it, yes," Mary answered, slightly annoyed at Ethel being referred to as 'the victim' rather than by her name. She knew, though, that she was partly to blame for this. All those episodes of *Her Law* she had appeared in where the victim was nothing more than someone to be killed off, depersonalised as a plot point.

"Well," Amy continued, "Why do you think she would have written that?"

"Maybe because it was true?" Mary answered.

"No! She was trying to deflect attention away from witchcraft wasn't she!"

Mary's mind joined the dots. "You think she was trying to get people to dismiss the idea of witchcraft in the area because she was a witch?" Mary said in a flat tone of voice which she hoped conveyed the ridiculousness of this idea.

"Well, it makes sense, doesn't it?" Amy said excitedly. "I mean, people around there think she's a witch, and rumours are going around and things. So she decides to write this little book that says there were never any witches around there and it was all a load of rubbish. Someone knows better though, someone who must have known about witches and how to deal with them. So they recreated the way the last which was killed in the village." She leaned back in her chair with a grin, apparently satisfied with her version of events.

Mary, however, thought the scenario was

ridiculous. There was Something that Amy had said that had interested her though.

"I've never heard any rumours of Ethel being a witch," she said, though this wasn't strictly true. Ethel herself had mentioned that villagers were likely to think she was a witch the day before she had died, but why?

"You haven't been around the village much until recently have you? We've heard from some good sources that it was well known in the village itself."

"And could you share the names of these sources?"

"No!" Amy said with a vigorous shake of her head. "That would be totally unethical."

"As opposed to slapping a picture of a poor, murdered woman on the front of your newspaper?" Mary said, rising from her chair. She had had enough of the enthusiastic Amy and her rather selective version of morality.

"Oh, come on," the girl answered, rising as well, "that was a great scoop for us! We're only a small paper, you know."

Mary said nothing but continued heading towards the door.

"So shall we schedule in time for an interview on your new business?" Amy called desperately, but Mary was already heading out the door.

CHAPTER FIFTEEN

They had barely walked back through the door of Blancham hall when Mary's phone buzzed in her pocket. She let Dot and Pea take the bags of shopping they had gathered while she had been in the Tanbury Gazette office through to the kitchen and lingered in the hall. Inspector Corrigan's name appeared on the screen of her mobile.

"Have you got any news?" She said as she answered.

"Hello Mary, it's nice to hear from you too," Corrigan said, his voice dripping with sarcasm.

"Well?" Mary continued, ignoring his tone.

"I thought I'd just call to let you know that I've solved your case."

Mary blinked. She had been expecting an update on the case, but not to hear it had been solved.

"You know who killed Ethel?"

"No, I said I'd solved *your* case. You know, the one you were supposed to be investigating before you decided to take on mine as well?"

"The vandalism? The message on The Lightning Tree?"

"Got it in one, we've got a confession and everything."

"Who was it?!" Mary snapped, annoyed both that Corrigan had beaten her to the punch, and also by him clearly enjoying the moment.

"It was Lilly Cooper."

Mary turned over this unexpected news in silence. Lilly Cooper lived in a large house at the bottom of a lane which led out of the village from behind the pub. Though she had a husband, John, he was away with his work in the oil industry so much, he was a rare sight in the village.

The thought that Lilly could have been behind the vandalism seemed incredible to Mary. She was a beautiful woman who dressed glamorously as her husband's wage allowed, but she was also quietly spoken and, in Mary's opinion, rather dull.

"Why on earth would Lilly do something like that?!"

"According to her, Ethel Long had been sending her threatening letters, and she wanted to scare her."

"By accusing her of being a witch?!" Mary said incredulously. "That's ridiculous."

"Maybe so, but that's the reason she's given. She says that everyone in the village knew that Ethel was a witch, so she wanted to scare her into thinking she could suffer the fate of Emily Blankforth."

Mary's eyebrows rose at the name of the woman who had died so long ago and started the rumours of the occult that surrounded The Lightning Tree.

"I see you've been reading up on our village."

"I have, the whole thing is ridiculous, but it's pretty obvious Ethel Long's murder is wrapped in the thing."

"And how did she do it? Burn those letters in?"

"Took a stepladder, climbed it, painted the words on in nail polish remover, and set light to it."

"Nail polish remover?"

"It's highly flammable apparently, who knew, eh?"

"So, do you think Lilly could have killed Ethel?" Mary asked, hardly believing she was even asking the question it was so ridiculous.

"No, as a matter of fact," Corrigan answered with a sigh. "She's got an alibi for the night of the murder, unfortunately."

"So they're not even linked?" Mary said, more to herself than to Corrigan. It had seemed so obvious that the two incidents would be linked. In all the time she had lived near the village, nothing had ever happened at The Lightning Tree other than the odd silly rumour and the pub using it for its advantage. For two incidents to occur in the space of two days, both with links to witchcraft, seemed too much of a coincidence. Corrigan seemed to agree.

"I know, it seems crazy. She says she's come forward because she doesn't want anyone to think the two incidents had anything to do with each other. She's got an alibi for the murder, so wanted to make sure her name was clear."

"Who or what is her alibi by the way?"

"Come on Mary, I can't tell you everything about the murder investigation, I just wanted to let you know that the vandalism mystery has been solved. Of course," he added, a smile reflected in his voice. "There's nothing to stop you going to speak to her yourself."

"You've released her?"

"As far as we can prove, she burned some letters into a tree and nothing else. We released her about half an hour ago with a warning. She wasn't being much use to us."

There was a pause as he left that thought lingering a moment.

"You're hoping I might have more luck," Mary said, catching on.

"Well I'd appreciate any more information you could pass on to aid in our investigation," he answered in a suddenly serious tone.

"Of course you would," Mary answered. "I'll be in touch."

She hung up before he could answer and frowned in thought.

CHAPTER SIXTEEN

Bloxley shone with a dull glow in the afternoon sun. Dappled shadows danced from the leaves of the oak trees that were dotted around the village. All of which paled in comparison to The Lightning Tree which sat at its heart.

As Pea guided the car passed the village green, Mary saw the upright figure of Reggie Downe, the vicar, exiting Copeland's butchers.

Mary noticed he was carrying nothing, so his visit had not been of a shopping nature.

"Pea," she said suddenly, "can you pull over?"

He pulled the car to a stop a hundred yards from where the vicar was making his way down the narrow pavement.

Mary turned in her seat to Dot, who was in the

back seat, looking at her as curiously as her brother was.

"Listen, Dot, you're not going to like this, but I think your old school friend knows a lot more about all this business than he's letting on. He had that argument with George Copeland in the pub that night, and he's just come out of the butchers with no meat. So he wasn't in there shopping."

"He's the vicar for goodness sake!" Dot snapped. "It's his job to talk to his parishioners!"

"I think Mary's right," Pea jumped in enthusiastically. "I knew there was something fishy about that chap the first moment I met him."

Dot narrowed her eyes at him, and he wilted under the gaze.

"Why don't you just go and have a chat to him about it all," Mary said, "then we can discount him as having anything to do with it."

Dot folded her arms.

"You want me to go and spy on a vicar, a friend, so you can rule him out as a murderer?"

"It's not spying! I just want you to talk to him, he'll open up to you."

The vicar appeared alongside the car, smiled in, and then checked his walk as he saw Dot through the window. He bent down and gave a little wave.

"I'll see you both later," Dot said, opening the door and climbing out to the pavement.

"Do you think that means she's going to do it?" Mary said as they watched Dot and the vicar walk off ahead.

"No idea, but I wish I'd realised you were going to send her off with him before I jumped in and backed you up."

"Oh, Pea, stop being such a jealous dope. He's an old school friend, that's all!"

"Hmm," Pea grumbled as he restarted the car and pulled out into the road. Dot glared at them as they passed her, while the vicar gave a little wave. Mary and Pea said nothing for a moment as he continued the car down the small road leading out of the village before taking a side road right.

"Is everything alright between you two?" Mary asked, breaking the silence.

"Oh fine, fine," Pea said distantly.

"Come on Pea, you can talk to me."

He sighed heavily. "I did something a bit silly and she got the hump with me that's all, I think she might be taking it out on me by cosying up with this vicar rotter."

"What did you do?"

"No time now," Pea said, "we're here."

The road was narrow, with either side of the tall, thick hedges being only inches from the sides of the car as the house appeared after a small bend in the track.

"I haven't been out here for years," Mary said.

"I had drinks with John a few months ago before he shot off again," Pea answered.

Mary frowned. She had never liked John Cooper. He was a loud, brash man who slapped his friends on the back a lot and gave lustful looks to any female within fifty yards. He worked in the oil industry, and as far as Mary could tell, only came home four or five times a year, where he'd throw small parties at their home. Lilly Cooper was always hovering in the background, playing the dutiful host while her husband held court.

The house itself consisted of red brick and, from the front at least, looked like a miniature version of Blancham Hall. Mary knew, though, that the similarities didn't last past the front door.

Inside, the house was sleek, modern, and in her mind, more like a show house than somewhere that people actually lived.

There was a small section of scaffolding standing on the right-hand side of the house. Maybe the outside was being modernised as well.

Within seconds of Pea ringing the bell, the door swung open, Lilly Cooper had clearly been expecting them.

"Mary, Pea," she said quietly, "Please, come in."

They followed her through to the hallway, its light grey floor tiles gleaming as though they had just been laid.

She offered them drinks which they declined, and soon they were seated at one end of the long living room, which led to the terrace and pool at the back of the house.

"I've already spoken to Frank at The Cauldron," Lilly said before either Mary or Pea could speak. "I explained that it was me that burned the message into the tree and that I was very sorry and that it wouldn't happen again."

"Right," Pea said, looking at Mary in slight confusion.

"He was very kind about it all and said that if anything, it was going to be good for business. He did ask if I would agree to say that your new investigating firm had discovered it was me, but I don't like to lie."

Mary sat blinking at her as she tried to process this.

She had known that the publicity of the apparently occult would be good for the pub, which is why she'd been suspicious of the landlord requesting them in the first place. Then she had realised her involvement would only generate more press coverage.

There was something in the way Lilly was talking, though. As if this was a speech she had been rehearsing, waiting for their arrival.

"That's all fine," Mary said. "But why did you do it at all? It seems so unlike you."

Lilly looked down as she brushed some imagined dust from her woollen skirt. "I feel quite embarrassed about it, I'm afraid I just lost my temper. I don't remember much about it. I was so angry."

"And this was because of a letter you'd had?" Pea asked. "One of these nasty ones that have been going around?"

She nodded. "Horrible, just horrible," she answered with a shudder. "But I just wanted to scare Ethel, just get her to stop sending them, I never imagined someone would kill her."

"Just a day later," Mary said, "quite a coincidence, don't you think?"

Lilly looked at her properly for the first time since they had arrived. Her pale blue eyes fixed on Mary's.

"Ethel Long was not a nice woman, but I would never wish that on anybody!"

"And luckily for you," Mary said, "you have an alibi for the night she was killed."

"Yes," Lilly answered, shifting in her seat, "and the police have checked up on it and are assured that I had nothing to do with it."

"So who were you with?"

"The police are satisfied." She said curtly. "I don't see the need for anyone else to be involved."

Mary narrowed her eyes at her. "Why don't you want to tell us?"

"As I said," Lilly said, attempting to make her quiet voice sound firm, "I don't think anyone else needs to be involved. The police have spoken to them. The gossip in this village is bad enough."

There was a moment of silence, with Mary hoping that Lilly would continue. Instead, she rose from her chair.

"I seem to have a headache coming on, so if you don't mind."

"Right, of course," Pea said rising.

Mary swallowed down the frustration of having a brother who complied so readily and allowed herself to be led out through the hallway and back onto the driveway where she turned back to Lilly.

"I know the police will have said this already, but if there's anything you can think of that might relate to Ethel's murder, anything at all."

Lilly's pale brow furrowed as her mouth opened and then closed again.

"As you say, the police have gone over everything. Goodbye, Mary, Pea." She closed the door leaving Mary feeling a strange discomfort as she headed back to the car.

CHAPTER SEVENTEEN

It was early evening when Dot returned to Blancham Hall. Hetty had come up from the village to cook, and she was just about serving when Dot arrived, shaking her coat off from the rain outside before hanging it on the large coat stand in the corner of the hall.

"You're back late," Mary said, as she emerged from the baize door which led through to the kitchens, Hetty close behind her and both holding trays laden with dishes.

"It's hardly late," Dot grumbled, showing Mary that she was still clearly disgruntled with her. "In any case, you're the one that sent me off on a spying mission against a friend of mine. A vicar no less!"

"Come on Dot, that's what we do now, isn't it? Investigate things!"

"And that means we trust no one? Suspect everyone?"

"Yes!" Mary laughed.

"You better not go suspecting me of anything young lady," Hetty chided.

"Oh, not you Hetty, you're an exception."

Hetty nodded with a self-satisfied smile before heading through into the dining room.

"Come on," Mary said to Dot. "You can fill us in on the vicar's dirty secrets over dinner."

Dot's lips pursed, but she followed Mary into the dining room anyway.

"Dot!" Pea cried, his face splitting into a grin as he rose at her entrance. "You alright? I was starting to get worried about you!"

"Starting to?" Hetty tutted as she lifted lids from the steaming dishes in the centre of the table. "He's been bouncing around like a cat on a hot tin roof all afternoon."

Pea grinned sheepishly, but Dot seemed to ignore him. Instead, she held her plate up as Hetty scooped a healthy portion of cottage pie onto her plate.

Mary decided to break the tension by relating her and Pea's visit to Lilly Cooper.

"I always that woman was an odd one," Hetty said enthusiastically when she'd finished. "Never trust the quiet ones, especially when they wear dresses that cost as much as that one does!"

Mary shifted uncomfortably as she thought of her own dress expenses.

"Still," she said, turning attention back to the vandalism, "it seems so out of character for her to do something like that."

"I'll tell you what you could do," Hetty said, "talk to Gloria Cotton and Beryl Copeland."

"Why's that?" Dot asked suddenly, as though the conversation that had so far passed her by had finally grabbed her attention.

"Those two have been thick as thieves for years, and Lilly's been hanging around with them more these last few months. No doubt she needs the company with her husband never home."

"You think Lilly might have talked to them about the letters?" Mary asked. "Or about burning the message into the tree?"

"No one else she could tell." Hetty shrugged. "John Cooper's been away for months."

Mary looked up at the others. Pea rarely spoke during mealtimes, preferring to focus on the task at hand which, for him, was always to consume as much as possible as fast as possible.

Dot though had a curious look about her. She

was poking at her plate, her face twisted in deep thought.

"What is it, Dot?" Mary asked, and remembering her friend's sudden interjection. "Is it something about Gloria and Beryl?"

Dot looked up at her sharply before her face softened with a sigh.

"Reggie said that there's been something strange going on between them for a few weeks."

"Strange how?" Mary asked.

"bviously Reggie can't betray any confidences."

"Obviously," Pea muttered, causing Dot to throw him a sharp look.

"But he did say that he had been concerned about both of them, Gloria in particular. She's been very upset by Ethel's death, apparently."

Hetty frowned. "That's odd, Gloria never had much time for Ethel when she was alive. Always said she was a nosy old witch." She looked up at them all, her mouth forming a perfect 'O'. "You don't think...?"

"Dot," Mary said, her voice urgent, "tell us exactly what the vicar said."

"He said that Gloria had come to him at the church, and she'd been distraught. He said that it was upsetting, of course, but that she shouldn't worry about her own safety as it was almost certainly the work of some lunatic passing through."

"That doesn't sound very much like goodwill to all men," Pea grumbled.

"He is talking about a murderer!" Dot shot back at him. "Anyway, apparently she wasn't upset because she was worried, she said she couldn't help feeling it was all her fault."

A thick silence fell around the table as everyone considered this.

"And your vicar chap hasn't told the police this?" Pea said crossly. "I have to say, I think that's a pretty poor show."

"He has to protect the wishes of his parishioners. They talk to him privately and expect him to be discreet."

"He's quite happy to go blabbing to you though," Pea retorted.

Mary decided to jump in before Dot could respond. "Surely he must have asked what she meant?"

"He did, but she wouldn't say. She just said she was probably being silly and to ignore her. He's spoken to her since and asked her to go to the police with anything she might know, but she said she didn't know anything."

Mary pictured Gloria Cotton's plump face as she had seen her in the shop on the day Ethel's body had been discovered. She had seemed uncomfortable, nervous. For that matter, so had her husband Charles, but that was to be expected. He had just found the body and the police were at their shop. For the first time, Mary wondered if there was anything else behind that nervousness.

"And did he have any news on anyone else?" Mary asked.

"He said Lilly Cooper had come to him about the vandalism and that he'd told her to do the right thing and go to the police. She was the one he'd been talking about the other day."

"She followed his advice at least," Mary said.

Dot nodded. "Lilly was in a bit of a state about it all and seemed to be worried about Gloria and Beryl."

"Worried about them?" Pea asked.

Dot shrugged. "I guess she was worried what they might think of her. She doesn't seem to have many friends, and if she was getting friendly with them, maybe she thought this would ruin it?"

"Ha!" Hetty barked sarcastically. "Those two would have bloody revelled in it! They love a bit of gossip and scandal."

"Either way," Mary said, pouring herself a large glass of red wine from the bottle on the table, "I think we should go and have a little chat with the two of them tomorrow."

CHAPTER EIGHTEEN

The sun was shining the next morning when Mary travelled into Bloxley. Pea had offered to drive, but the frosty silence that hung between him and Dot over breakfast had caused her to snap. She had demanded they both stay at the house and talk to each other before she banged their heads together.

She wondered, as she headed down the small lane lined with tall hedges which led to the village, how she had ever lived in London for so long. She still loved the city of course, and she would be lying if she said she didn't miss some aspects of the glitz and glam of her never-ending social life there, but so much had changed in her life in such a short space of time that she was a different person now. She had changed, she was changing, but how or into what, she wasn't sure. The countryside though had beguiled her again, as it had done in her youth. Right now, it was easy to see why.

The birdsong was so numerous as to almost be deafening, the soft morning light seemed like soft butter filling the lane as bees swam through it lazily.

This peaceful slice of the English countryside was suddenly pierced by a horn sounding on the lane ahead. Mary pressed herself into the hedge and waited for the vehicle which appeared around the corner at some speed. Before screeching to a halt next to her.

"Mary Blake!" A voice said as the window wound down. "Just the person I was coming to see!"

Mary moved across and bent down to see the smirking face of the reporter Matt Sharpe.

"And what would you want me for Mr Sharpe?" Mary said, placing her hands on her hips and standing upright.

"Just delivering a bit of post I thought you would be interested in." He grinned as he turned to the passenger seat. He retrieved a newspaper and held it out towards Mary.

She took it with a sudden sense of dread. Whatever had led to the smug look on his face, she was sure it wasn't good.

"You'll be glad to know you're still front-page material," he continued, "I mean, it's only the

Tanbury Gazzette, but I'd imagine you need to take what you can get these days. Am I right?"

He gave a small chuckle before throwing the car into reverse and moving back down the lane until he could turn in the gateway of field and head back the way he had come.

Mary unfolded the paper and stared down at her face. The picture was not a flattering one. Taken a few years ago when a particularly aggressive photographer had been shoving his camera in her face as she was leaving a nightclub. She had been wild with fury, and the picture showed it. She snarled out from the front page of the Tanbury Gazette with her hair a mess, her eyes crazed and her makeup smudged. This wasn't even the worst thing about the papers front page. That was saved for the headline.

'*COULD FADED TV STAR HAVE MADE A DEADLY BID TO REGAIN STARDOM?*'

Mary's eyes widened as she read the attached article. Matt Sharpe had written the piece, and it dripped with the arrogance and smugness of his personality. It talked about how Mary had been in close proximity to two suspicious deaths since her tv career had fallen flat. Neatly failing to mention her role in bringing both killers to justice. It mentioned her 'suspiciously close' relationship with Inspector Joe Corrigan, implying how useful this was to avoid suspicion. Then, the meat of the story.

He had written that Mary had been seen visiting the victim the day before and that she had no alibi for the night of the murder. Wrapping up with a neat paragraph or two on how she had become obsessed with trying to recreate the role of a detective she had played on tv, in real life before ending with the cutting line,

'How many have to die around Mary Blake before someone questions her involvement?'

He had painted her as someone unstable, someone who was obsessed with death and murder and who wanted the fame she had enjoyed back at all costs. He had implied she was a killer.

She rolled the newspaper up and clenched it in her fist as she continued her walk towards the village, the birdsong now drowned out by the sound of her blood rushing in her ears.

CHAPTER NINETEEN

B y the time Mary had reached the village, her anger had subsided to a mere simmer. That was until she saw the sign that stood outside the post office that held the day's headline. She marched towards it and pulled the sheet of paper out from under the mesh that held it, tearing it as she did so. She scrunched it into a ball and marched on the shop, pushing the door open so hard that the small bell above it was almost ripped from its fixing.

Gloria Cotton looked up from behind the counter with a look of complete panic on her face.

"I can't believe you are putting this rubbish up!" Mary shouted, slamming the ball of paper on the counter, making several pens that Gloria was stuffing into a plastic bag jump to the floor.

"I'm sorry, Mary," Gloria said, her face flushed.

"But we've got to put the paper out. We always put the paper out!"

"Even when it's full of nonsense like this?!"

Gloria said nothing for a moment before bending to pick up the fallen pens and continuing to add them to the bag. She looked tired and harassed. Dark patches circled her eyes which looked puffy, as though she had been crying.

Dot's words rang through Mary's mind. The vicar had said that Gloria had been distraught at Ethel's murder, even saying that she felt responsible somehow.

"I'm sorry Gloria, I know it's not your fault," Mary said as she bent to pick up the pens that had fallen on her side of the counter before handing them over.

"Thank you," Gloria said meekly, continuing to stuff the bag.

"Is everything ok?" Mary said.

Gloria's small, rounded eyes locked on to hers, and Mary was suddenly struck with the impression that these were frightened eyes. Terrified eyes.

"Are you in some kind of trouble?" Mary said quietly, leaning over the counter and placing her hand on Gloria's. "If you tell me, I might be able to help."

"Oh Mary," she said in a shaky voice, "I did

something so foolish, and now it's caused all this mess, and poor Ethel!"

"Gloria, if you know something about what happened to her, it will be better for you if you tell me. I can help you go to the police."

Gloria's eyes widened. "No! I can't!" She shook her head violently as she stepped back from the counter.

"Everything all right?" Charles's voice came from the back of the shop. His eyes darted from his wife, who was still looking at Mary with an expression of horror. To Mary, whose annoyance at the interruption was clearly visible on her face.

"Ah, I'd imagine this is about the headline on the Gazette today?" Charles said nodding to himself and stroking his moustache as he made his way through the shop. "I'm sorry Mary, I know it's an unfair piece, but we don't get to decide when we can sell it or not."

"It's fine," Mary said dismissively, all thoughts of the article gone entirely from her mind now. "I just wanted to make sure you and Gloria were ok."

Charles frowned for a moment and then smiled. "Yes, quite over my little shock at finding poor Ethel thank you. Though Gloria here seems to be making a bit of a meal of it!" His light chuckle was cut off midway when he saw the expression on his wife's face more closely. "Are you ok, Gloria?"

"I'm fine," she snapped in return, thrusting the last of the pens into a bag and moving out from behind the counter.

"Goodbye, Mary," Gloria said, "thanks for your concern, but we're both fine."

She stared fiercely at Mary, making it clear she expected her to leave. The fear was still etched on her face, but it had a hardness to it now. She was trying to face up to whatever it was that had gripped her.

Mary took a pen that Gloria had missed from the counter and wrote her mobile number on a notepad.

"If you want to talk," she said, sliding the notepad across before turning towards the door. She opened the shop door and stepped out onto the street as she heard Charles questioning why Gloria was throwing away perfectly good pens.

She took a deep lungful of fresh air and looked down the street both ways. As she looked to her left towards the village green and the lightning tree, she saw a figure coming towards her. Recognising Beryl Copeland, butcher George Copeland's wife and friend of Gloria, she seized her chance to talk to her away from the shop by marching to meet her.

"Hello Mary," she said with a sweet smile. She adjusted the thick-lensed glasses, which perched on her nose.

"Beryl, just the person I was looking for!"

"Oh?" she said, glancing behind Mary towards the shop. "Is everything ok with Gloria?"

"She seems quite upset about Ethel's death," Mary replied.

Beryl frowned. "Yes, I was actually on my way to check in on her. She's been very upset."

"Why is that do you think?"

Beryl shot her shocked glance.

"I mean," Mary continued, "Obviously, it's upsetting for everyone, no one deserves to die like that."

"Well, maybe so," Beryl said, "but I dare say Gloria has reason to be glad that Ethel isn't around anymore."

Now it was Mary's turned to look shocked.

"What on Earth makes you say that?!"

Beryl's lips pursed, and her eyes narrowed. "It's not my place to spread gossip, that was Ethel's department. All I'll say is, Gloria had good reason to not be too sad at Ethel's passing as did many others in this village. Now I better be getting to Gloria and see how she is."

She gave a curt nod and passed Mary on the narrow pavement, heading to the shop.

Mary decided to buy more steaks.

CHAPTER TWENTY

"Mary! Back already?"

"Yes, George, Percy sent me for more steaks. Same again please!" She said with what she hoped was her most winning smile.

"Right you are," he chuckled as he began to fetch the steaks from inside the counter.

"I just bumped into Beryl outside, she seems very worried about Gloria."

George's hand hesitated in wrapping the first cut of meat and then continued.

"I don't know what's got into her recently," he said, shaking his head. "She's been all over the place for weeks."

"And this is because of Gloria?"

"Those two have always been thick as thieves, but don't ask me what goes on between them, I wouldn't have a clue. I know Gloria's got her fretting though, keeps going on about how she needs to be there for her and how I wouldn't understand. Seems to be more than happy to chat away to that bloody vicar though." He looked up at Mary suddenly, as though he had only just realised she was there. "Sorry, ignore me. All this business in the village has just got everyone on edge."

"From what I've heard, the village has been on edge for a while anyway." He placed the wrapped steaks in a bag and passed them over the counter before moving to the till. "You know, because of the letters?" Mary pressed as she handed him her bank card.

"You got one too, eh? Nasty stuff." He shuddered as he handed back her card. "At least that's one good thing to come out of this I suppose."

"Sorry, what is?"

"Well, the letters will stop, won't they?"

She frowned. "You think Ethel was writing the letters?"

"Had to have been," he shrugged, "she always did have her nose stuck in other people's business."

"And you think that was why she was killed?"

"I don't know about that," he said, shifting nervously. "I mean, the letters weren't nice, but killing someone like that?"

"What other reason would there be?"

George's thin lips twisted as though he chewed on something sour. "Depends on what you believe I guess," he said, "a lot of people thought Ethel was messing with the occult, you know."

"You mean people thought she was a witch?"

He shrugged. "You saw the message on the tree."

"Written by a human, not some spirit," Mary said, knowing that news of Lilly Cooper's artsy would have long got around the village.

"Yeah, but who knows what drove Lilly to do something like that? She's not really the type is she?"

"Are you suggesting she was possessed or something?" Mary said, unable to hide how ridiculous she found all of this.

"I'm just saying it was out of character and that tree has a history," he answered, somewhat defensively. "Anyway, I best get on," he said, with a tone that suggested their conversation was over. Mary decided that she had already lost her audience and so decided there was no harm in pushing it.

"You know, if there's anything you might know about Ethel's death, you have to tell somebody. If not the police, then me."

"Why would I know anything?"

"It's a small village, George, everyone knows something."

He didn't answer immediately. Instead, he folded his arms and pursed his lips as he took a deep breath in through his nose.

"There were plenty who'd had enough of Ethel around here, but I don't know anyone from this village who would have killed her."

"I guess I'll just have to believe in some sort of spirit who hangs around the village waiting for a witch to murder then won't I?" she said, her frustration getting the better of her.

The shop door opened behind her and a man Mary didn't recognise walked in.

"Phillip!" George said in surprise. "I wasn't expecting you." He gestured to Mary. "Mary, this is Phillip Laslow, Beryl's cousin. Phillip, this is Mary Blake."

"I liked your show," the man smiled.

"Thank you," Mary said curtly. "Goodbye, George."

She left the shop, the bag of steaks swinging at her side, and marched down the street without caring where she was going. Just a short time ago, she had been feeling as though she belonged here again. That she was finally finding her feet after her acting career had been unceremoniously ended. But in the last few hours, she had been branded a suspected murderer by the local paper. She had Gloria refuse her offer of help despite clearly being in a state over something. To top it all, the local butcher was more inclined to believe in witchcraft and mysticism than cold-blooded murder.

She paused as a large shadow looked over her. She looked up at The Lightning Tree, its brooding shape dark against the bright white cloud above.

Why had all this nonsense started up again? She had heard the stories as a child, but it was just a local legend. She couldn't believe that Ethel's death could have anything to do with the rumours of her being a witch, it had to be about those letters. Which would mean that all this rubbish about the tree was just a distraction. Someone using the old legend to cover something else, or at least to muddy the waters enough to have people looking in the wrong direction.

The trouble was, everyone in the village would have known legends, and so anyone could have used them. She thought about the symbols found chalked on Ethel's body. A move so cold and calculated if they were to muddy the investigation. She pictured the killer, standing over the small, frail body of the woman they had just murdered, and calmly drawing the symbols on before leaving her there in the hollow of the tree. She jumped as her phone buzzed in her pocket. It was Pea.

"Are you still in the village?"

"Yes, why?"

"I've just found out something interesting about our new vicar. We'll meet you at the green in five minutes."

The line went dead, but Mary knew from Pea's excited tone that he had discovered something that painted the vicar in an altogether different light from the glowing one Dot saw him in.

CHAPTER TWENTY-ONE

Mary knew the gossip was going to be juicy
as soon as the car had pulled up and Dot
and Pea had clambered out. Dot's faced was pinched
in a half grimace, while Pea was clearly trying to keep
a smile from his face.

"You're not going to believe it!" Pea said with
barely disguised glee.

"I'm not sure I do yet," Dot grumbled beside him.

"Come on Dot, you heard the man!"

"Less bickering, more explaining," Mary said
impatiently.

"You remember I'd put out the feelers on the
vicar? Something about the chap I didn't trust."

"I can't think why," Mary said, glancing at Dot
who reddened slightly.

"I finally heard back from a friend of mine who

knows something who knows someone who works for the local paper near his old parish."

Mary ignored trying to follow this trail and instead just urged him on with a nod of her head.

"Apparently he left under quite a cloud, left the whole village in an uproar! The church moved him on quickly, tried to stick him somewhere quiet where he wouldn't cause any more trouble, and I think we can see how that turned out?" He said, eyebrows rising.

"Oh, for heaven's sake!" Dot snapped. "None of this means he had anything to do with the murder!"

"Maybe not," Pea conceded, "but you can't deny it's a bit fishy that he hasn't mentioned any of this."

"It's hardly something you would go around talking about, is it?" Dot muttered.

"Can you two stop bickering and tell me what the hell is going on?!" Mary said, waving her hands in the air in exasperation.

"Right, sorry," Pea said, probably sensing Mary was liable to whack him soon if he didn't start spilling. "From what I heard, our new vicar is a bit of a ladies' man! Sounds like he had his way with half the women in the town!"

Dot tutted at this, her cheeks reddening further, but said nothing.

"Anyway," Pea continued, "there was a certain

amount of local scandal about it when one irate husband clocked the vicar across the jaw at a fundraising event."

"Blimey!" Mary began to laugh, before cutting it short under Dot's gaze. "So, there's a chance he might have been up to his old tricks here?"

"Who knows," Pea answered with a broad grin, "but it made me wonder if that's what the argument in the pub we heard of was about."

"With George Copeland," Mary said thoughtfully.

"Exactly." Pea folded his arms with a satisfied expression on his face, "It wouldn't surprise me if his wandering eye was behind all of this."

"Come on Pea," Mary said, even before Dot had reacted. "I can't see how the vicar putting himself about a bit would result in Ethel's death."

"Maybe she found about his indiscretions?" Pea offered. "And he decided to keep her quiet?"

Mary opened her mouth to say how ridiculous this was but then paused. Maybe Pea had a point? If the vicar had lost one of his posts already due to indiscretion, what would happen if he had another misdemeanour in the eyes of the church? If his career was at risk, maybe he would have gone to extreme lengths to save it? Including silencing Ethel Long.

If anyone in the village was likely to have known

about something like an illicit affair, it would have been Ethel.

"I can't believe Reginald would have done something like that," Dot said quietly.

The fight seemed to have gone out of her now, and Mary noticed that she had referred to her old school friend as Reginald and not Reggie. Something had changed there.

"In any case," Dot continued, "I'm sure the police will know all about it and have probably dismissed it as nonsense already."

"Maybe so, but Corrigan didn't mention it," Mary said. "I think it's best we ask the vicar directly, don't you? Why don't you invite him to lunch at the pub?"

Dot's eyes flashed with annoyance for a split second at being used again. Before she sighed, nodded, and pulled out her phone. She turned away to make the call and Pea raised his eyebrows at Mary.

"Quite the turn up isn't it? It certainly gives us a reason to put the vicar in as suspect number one."

Mary took a deep breath and looked up at the lightning tree nearby. "I'm not sure it does, there are too many other things going on here."

"What do you mean?"

"There's all this witchcraft nonsense for starters," Mary replied.

"But we know it was Lily Cooper who did all that," Pea said. "She's the one who burnt the message in the tree after all."

"Yes, but she wasn't the one who chalked those symbols on Ethel's clothes after she was killed was she? At least the police don't think so, because she had an alibi. So someone else must have been wrapped up in this witchcraft nonsense as well." As she said this, her mind flashed back to the butchers' shop and her conversation with George Copeland. He had undoubtedly been convinced that was an element of the occult at play in the village.

"And that's not all," she continued, bringing her mind back to her topic, "there are the letters to think about."

Pea shrugged, "Maybe the vicar was behind those as well? They only started being sent in the last six months or so didn't they? After he arrived?"

"For heaven's sake," Dot muttered as she rejoined them, "now Reginald's been sending nasty letters as well, has he?"

"I'm just saying he could have done," Pea said in a quiet voice.

"Are we on for lunch in the pub?" Mary asked.

Dot nodded. "He'll meet us there."

"Then what are we waiting for? Let's go and get a table."

CHAPTER TWENTY-TWO

The Cauldron was more lively than Mary had seen it in years. She realised that a murder that played on the theme of witchcraft was good for business, as she had suspected. She looked across the busy pub to Frank Roach. He had greeted them warmly, unnaturally so if anything. At first, she had assumed that her presence was just another thing that was going to boost business, now though, she wondered. Was he being overly lovely because he was worried they were onto him? Would he really have committed such a brutal act just to improve business at the pub?

She shook herself free from the thought. She was getting paranoid, and she needed to snap out of it, or her mind would never be clear enough to actually think this through.

"Are you ok, Mary?" Dot asked.

"Yes, sorry. Miles away."

"Here comes the love god himself," Pea said quietly, nodding towards the door.

They looked up to see the vicar in the opening of the front door, his eyes gazing around the room. As they landed on them, in particular Dot, he beamed and gave a jolly wave.

"Hello!" he said with a chuckle, rubbing his hands together. "Can I get everyone a refresh?"

"I'll give you a hand," Mary said, rising from the table. "We can order lunch at the same time."

"Excellent," he smiled and opened his arm up to allow her to lead the way. As she passed him, his hand came to rest on the small of her back to guide her passed. An innocent enough gesture, particularly from a vicar, if she hadn't just heard of his reputation as a womaniser.

They reached the bar, and she relayed their drinks orders. She watched him as he attempted to catch the eye of either Frank or Allie Crowther who was also working behind the bar.

He wasn't what Mary would have considered an attractive man. His round face accentuated by the round glasses were pleasant enough, but not something that would have screamed 'ladies' man'.

"Business seems to be doing well!" he said once

the drinks were ordered. He looked around at the pub's clientele with a mild-mannered grin.

"Murder seems to bring out the sightseers," Mary agreed.

His smile flickered and then vanished.

"Oh, right."

There drinks arrived, delivered by Frank who barely acknowledged them in the rush to serve. They ordered lunch and returned to the table where Dot sat, straight-backed and purse-lipped and Pea lolled his lengthy frame in his chair with the air of someone who was about to enjoy himself.

"I'm afraid Reginald," Mary began, deciding to get straight to business.

"Reggie, please," the vicar said, holding his left hand up as he sipped at his beer.

"Ok, Reggie," Mary continued. "I'm afraid we have heard some things about why you left your previous post."

The smile vanished instantly, and his eyes flicked to Dot, who studiously avoided his gaze.

"I left my post because I felt I had done all I could there, I needed a change."

"So it wasn't because half the town's husbands wanted to knock your block off?" Pea laughed until Dot elbowed him in the ribs.

There was a pause as the vicar stared at his drink, slowly turning it in his hands.

"Well," he said eventually, looking up at them all, the mild-mannered grin back on his face, "it seems you have been looking into my background. Can I ask why?"

"There's been a murder in the village," Mary said in a flat tone.

Reggie's eyebrows shot up as though he'd been electrocuted. "You think I had something to do with Ethel's death?!"

"Maybe she found out why you had been moved on from your last post?" Mary shrugged. Now she was saying it out loud, it seemed less convincing than she had initially thought. Had she merely been caught up in Pea's excitement at finding out the vicar wasn't quite as squeaky clean as Dot had felt?

"I feel I hardly need to say it," Reggie continued, looking pointedly at Dot who was turning a deep crimson, "but I had nothing to do with Ethel's death."

"We didn't really think you did," Dot said hurriedly, "we were just trying to be thorough."

"I jolly well wasn't," Pea bristled. "Seems like it might well be something you'd want to be kept quiet. Are you telling us that you were ok with Ethel blabbing all over the village that more often than not you have your trousers round your ankles?!"

"I'll ignore that," the vicar smiled sweetly. "Who says she even knew?"

"Ethel Long? Of course she knew! She made it her business to know everything about everybody. Until someone bashed her over the head, of course."

The exchange had been fast, almost aggressive. As though the two men were trading blows rather than talking. It was Reggie who seemed to be on the losing end.

"Ok," he said, his voice smaller than it had been, "you're right, there didn't seem to be anything that woman didn't know."

He seemed to realise he had spoken out of turn and checked himself. "Ethel I mean, I liked her. She was a very strong-willed woman."

Mary wasn't buying his apparent affection for Ethel. She had heard the tone when he said the words 'that woman', they all had.

Reggie seemed to realise he was losing his audience. He leaned back, sagging in his seat as he exhaled slowly.

"Ok, ok," he said softly. "I guess you deserve the truth." He leaned forward and looked at Dot, the smile returning. "Especially you Dot, you deserve better than being lied to."

Mary saw it now, saw how he'd had so much success with women. He was just so calm, so softly spoken, and so damned inoffensive. In his role as vicar, he could become a confidant, someone who the bored and troubled housewife could turn to for comfort, and eventually, something more. He was a human comfort blanket.

"The truth is," he continued, "that not only did Ethel Long know about my previous troubles, but she was intent on torturing me with them. She sent me letters, describing how she knew all my dirty little secrets." He gave a small chuckle at this and shook his head. "None of it is as bad as it sounds, Dot."

She gave a small shrug in reply but said nothing.

"In any case, in the first week I moved here Ethel made it very clear she knew all about why I was posted out. She made it clear that I wasn't to go causing trouble in 'her' village. Though I think it's pretty clear that she was the troublemaker."

"Because she warned you not to cause trouble?" Mary asked.

"No, because of the letters. Don't tell me none of you got them?"

"No, we didn't."

"You must be the only ones in the village who didn't."

"And you think it was Ethel writing them?"

"Of course it was! Everyone knew it, I don't know why they put up with it."

"Someone decided not to," Pea said pointedly.

"Yes, but not me!" Reggie said, exasperated. "You can ask the police, I have an alibi for the night she was killed."

"Lily Cooper," Mary said, surprising herself as much as anyone. She looked at his shocked expression, and knew she had hit home. "You were with her the night Ethel was killed, that's why they let her go after the vandalism charge."

Reggie glanced at Dot briefly before his eyes returned to Mary's. "Lily is a lonely woman, I was comforting her that night as she had been particularly down."

"Comforting her!" Pea snorted.

"And what about the night before," Mary continued, "were you with Lily when she burnt the message into the tree?"

"No, I wasn't. If I had been, I would have stopped her, of course."

"Of course," Mary repeated slowly, holding his eye for a moment. "She must have talked to you about it though, you spent the next night with her."

"She was agitated, she'd received letters as well. I think she just snapped. I encouraged her to go to the police afterwards, which she did."

"Eventually," Mary nodded. "What about before, she didn't talk to you about what she was planning?"

"No, of course not! I would have stopped her."

"It's all quite a coincidence," Dot said, speaking for the first time. The others around the table stared at her, waiting for more. "You move here under a cloud, hoping that no one here will find out. No doubt planning to make your moves on the women of this village just like you did at your last." Reggie shifted in his seat and took a large gulp of his drink, but said nothing.

"But then," Dot continued, "as soon as you get here you meet Ethel, and she knows all about it because she was the kind of woman who liked to know things about people. Then you start receiving letters which refer to your past. You start getting friendly with Lily Cooper and then within a short time she's sneaking out in the night to commit threatening vandalism. Something that seems quite out of character for her. Then, a day later, the target of that message, Ethel Long, is killed underneath the same tree."

"Almost everyone in the village had letters," Reggie protested, "and believe me, people were angry about it."

"And how do you know other people were getting letters?" Pea asked.

Reggie squirmed in his seat. "I'm the vicar, people like to confide in me."

"The week before Ethel was killed," Mary asked, "there was an argument in here on Friday night, you were involved."

"Exactly my point!" Reggie said enthusiastically. "That was George Copeland, he was furious about getting nasty letters as well."

"But why was he angry with you?" Dot asked.

"There was a misunderstanding. He seemed troubled by something, and so I asked if he'd received any nasty letters. He got angry thinking I had had something to do with it, but I set him straight."

"By blaming Ethel Long?"

"I told him who I thought was sending them, yes." Reggie sat upright in his seat, raising his chin defiantly. "I would never wish something like that on anyone, but if you do evil in the world, it's no surprise that evil then seeks you out in return."

There was an uncomfortable pause which was eventually broken by Alice Crowther arriving with their lunch.

"Ham, egg, and chips?" She said, holding one of the plates aloft.

"Mine," claimed Pea, his eyes widening at the sight of food.

"And the fish finger sandwich?"

"Mine, thank you," the vicar said in a weak voice.

"I'll just get the others," Alison said, turning away.

"Alison?" Mary called, causing her to spin back to them. She had decided to take a punt on something that had just occurred to her. "We were just talking about how the vicar was the one who let Robert know that it was Ethel sending him the letters."

Her bright eyes flicked to Reggie's face. "I think it was pretty obvious it was Ethel anyway." She shrugged.

"Of course." Mary smiled back at her.

She looked confused for a second and then smiled back. "I'll just the rest of your food."

Mary turned to Reggie once she had gone. "It seems like quite a few people got the idea that Ethel was behind the letters from you vicar?"

"As Alison said, I think that most people would have come to that conclusion," he muttered into his beer.

"Yet it seems as though you gave them all a nudge," Mary countered.

"Do you know," Reggie said, drawing the last of his drink, "I think I ought to take this sandwich to go, I need to prepare for Ethel Long's funeral."

"Of course," Mary said, exchanging glances with

both Dot and Pea. "Wait, funeral? That's a bit soo,n isn't it?"

"Her daughter is in Scotland on business, she lives in Australia you see. So she's coming down to have it tomorrow before she goes back. I'll be seeing you all there, I trust?"

"We'll be there," Mary answered.

He gave a weak smile and scurried for the door, holding his sandwich wrapped in a paper serviette.

"That is not the air of an innocent man," Pea declared before stuffing a colossal lump of ham and eggs into his mouth.

Mary watched Dot, who simply pursed her lips and stared at the door until Alison arrived back with the salads that they had both ordered.

"Where's the vicar?" she asked as she laid their plates down.

"He had to rush off, tomorrow is Ethel's funeral."

Alison nodded sadly. "I think the whole village is going to turn out."

"Even though everyone thinks she was writing them these letters?"

Alison shrugged. "She still didn't deserve that," she frowned. "Wait, do you think someone else sent the letters?"

"I don't know," Mary replied, "but it seems as

though the vicar is the source of the rumours that Ethel wrote them, and they started after he arrived."

Alison's face turned to a shocked 'O', and she retreated behind the bar where Mary watched her whispering to Frank.

"That should stir the pot a bit," she said to the others before turning her attentions to her lunch.

CHAPTER TWENTY-THREE

Mary leaned back in her chair and watched the thinning crowd in the pub. Dot and Pea had returned to Blancham, but she had decided it was time to grill Corrigan on whatever information the police might have uncovered that they hadn't. There was the added incentive that she would get to see him alone.

Their few dates had been stilted, awkward affairs, and with the close proximity of the case to her family home, communications and now faltered as well. She had been surprised to realise how much she missed him.

As she had sat listening to Dot and Pea squabble over the likelihood of the vicar being a poison letter writing maniac or just a misguided sex fiend, she had realised that she wanted to see Corrigan. She wanted to be close enough to someone to bicker, to get on each other's nerves. And so, she had called him and asked him to come to The Cauldron. Since then, she found herself getting nervous, and she had no idea why. She never found cause to be shy of any man before. She had always been the one who was in control.

Now, she was regretting the third double gin she had ordered as the door opened and Corrigan's crooked smile and tousled hair appeared in the doorway. He waved over to her and headed to the bar where he ordered a pint of beer and to Mary's horror, another gin and tonic for her.

"How are you?" he said as he reached her table. "I saw the piece in the paper today."

"A proper hatchet job," she sighed, "it looks like I've got an enemy in the press."

He looked at her quizzically, and she explained about her encounter with Matt Sharpe.

"Maybe I should have a word with him?" Corrigan said gruffly.

"Very gallant of you." She smiled. "But I can fight my own battles, thank you.

What you can do is help me solve this case so I can put this reporter back in his box and get my business off to a good start." She looked at the smirk that had spread across Corrigan's face. "And find a killer of course, and get justice for Ethel Long."

"I'm glad you added those last two." Corrigan smiled.

Mary reached for the gin and tonic he had bought her and drank deeply, hoping this would cover up the blush she had felt rush to her cheeks.

"We haven't made much progress, to be honest," Corrigan sighed. "After we brought Robert Woods in everything's gone cold. We've been asking everyone in the village if they'd received any of the poison pen letters, but no one's opening up."

"There's something I can help you with," Mary said with not an insignificant amount of glee. "I can tell you now that the vicar, Reginald Downe, received some."

"Did he now?" Corrigan said, his thick eyebrows rising. "He certainly didn't mention that to us, and I bet I know what they were about as well."

"The reason he got moved on from his last posting," Mary finished for him.

He looked surprised again. "You have been busy, haven't you?"

"A little." Mary shrugged. "But we still only know reasons for two of the people who received them. Robert Woods was being accused of killing his parents. A strong enough motive I guess, but I don't think there's any real suggestion he did?"

"None," Corrigan confirmed. "We've been over the accident report. I think it was an empty threat intended to rile him, but who knows why?"

"And then there's the vicar, who was keen to keep his scandals behind him. Do we think that's a good enough reason for murder?"

"He lied about it." Corrigan shrugged. "People react in strange ways when their reputation is threatened."

"They do, but not him," Mary said thoughtfully. "He strikes me as someone who just rolls with the punches and carries on regardless."

"The only other person we know about is Lily Cooper, and although she took some sort of revenge with the graffiti, I don't buy her as the killer. She has an alibi in any case."

"From the vicar, who seems to be back to his old ways already."

Corrigan laughed. "So that's another thing you know already. Ok, so who else do you know received letters?"

"Charles Cotton and George Copeland did."

"And it was Charles who discovered the body," Corrigan said thoughtfully.

"I take it neither of them mentioned to the police that they had had letters either?"

"No, they didn't. The trouble with getting to the bottom of blackmail is the person being blackmailed. They rarely want the police to investigate if the reason for the blackmail is illegal."

Mary leaned back in her seat with a frown. She felt as if something had just clicked into place, or rather, out of place.

"None of them mentioned money," she said in a flat tone, as though reading from a script that had appeared in her mind from nowhere. "Everyone who has mentioned the letters has only said that they were nasty, threatening. There hasn't been a single mention of the letters asking for money at all."

"That doesn't mean they didn't though, maybe people just didn't want to admit that they'd paid someone off?"

"Maybe," Mary said unconvinced.

"Put it this way, why would anyone send letters like that to half the village if it wasn't for money?"

"Around here? Maybe just for something to do." She laughed, but he didn't join her.

"I thought you liked it here? You seemed more...settled."

"I do," Mary said, wondering why she had made

the jibe. "I just...wasn't expecting all this on my doorstep," she said, taking a deep breath.

"This is the game you're in now you know," Corrigan said softly. "Now you're in the investigation business, cases are going to come to you."

"I know, but murder? Here in Bloxley? I'm just not sure I was ready for it."

"I can't believe I'm hearing this from Mary Blake," Corrigan smiled. "I would have thought she was ready for anything."

She caught his eye and held it for a moment. "Maybe I'm not as strong as you think I am?" She said quietly.

"Oh, I know you are Mary," he answered, taking her hand. "You just need to realise that needing someone else isn't a sign of weakness."

CHAPTER TWENTY-FOUR

M ary woke to the shrill, business-like tone of a mobile phone ring that she knew wasn't her own. For a moment, she was disorientated until she heard a familiar deep groan in the bed beside her. She turned to see Corrigan, his mop of dark brown hair in even more disarray than usual, reaching for his phone.

"Corrigan," he grunted as he put the device to his ear. His body jerked upright. "When?"

Mary was alert now, feeling the sudden tension in his body. She gave a small involuntary shiver, but it wasn't from the cold.

"I'm on my way," Corrigan said, hanging up and leaping from the bed.

"What is it?" Mary asked, sitting upright.

"There's been another death," Corrigan answered as he pulled his white shirt over his head. "Apparently, our killer has committed suicide."

CHAPTER TWENTY-FIVE

The village was a scene of chaos once more. A hearse and another black car were parked at the side of the village green, three men dressed in black leaning on them and watching the stream of cars and people that were passing.

"Oh, my goodness!" Mary cried. "I'd forgotten about the funeral today."

"That's not going to go ahead now," Corrigan growled. "They'll have to wait until tomorrow."

Mary glanced at him as he steered the car past the green. He had been in a foul mood since the phone call, so different from how he had been last night. She allowed herself a moment to remember his soft kisses, his strong embrace.

Now though, he was all annoyance and short-tempered aggression. Someone else had died, and it appeared he would be robbed of the chance at bringing a killer to justice. The 'right kind' of justice he had said as they'd hurried down to the car. The kind that people could feel that the law had been upheld. Not another death with no answers.

Mary herself was still reeling. Gloria Cotton, the diminutive shopkeeper, was dead, apparently by her own hand. The police suspected an overdose. The most alarming bit of news, though, was that her suicide note had included a confession.

Mary thought back to her conversation with Gloria just yesterday and the fear and anger she had seen in her eyes.

Corrigan pulled the car up to the side of a shop where space had been left for him between two squad cars. An officer standing outside of the shop pulled himself upright as Corrigan stepped out of the vehicle.

Corrigan looked across at Mary, who had joined him on the pavement. "You shouldn't come in," he said in a low voice.

"Come on, Joe, I might be able to help. I'm coming whatever, it's not as if he's going to stop me." She jerked her thumb at the young officer who blinked at her in surprise. "No offence," she added.

"Um, none taken," the officer stammered.

Corrigan sighed, "Fine, but don't touch anything,"

"Obviously." Mary rolled her eyes at him. "I've been at hundreds of crime scenes, you know."

"Yes, but only two real ones," Corrigan reminded her.

They stepped through into the shop and were immediately confronted with the dead body of Gloria Cotton, slumped across the shop counter to their left.

"Wait here," Corrigan said in a tone that suggested he expected to be obeyed. He moved across to another uniformed officer who seemed to be positioned as far away from the body as possible. His gaze never landing on it for a moment. Even as Corrigan murmured questions at him and gestured back to the scene.

Mary herself was transfixed. Gloria lay, her head on the side as though she were sleeping, her closed eyes only adding to the sensation. She looked peaceful. To her left on the counter was a handwritten note, which Mary moved two steps closer and craned her neck to read.

I am confessing to the writing of numerous notes to people in the village of Bloxford

which contained any number of nasty and
vicious rumours and lies. I am so sorry
about poor Ethel, but

AND THERE THE note ended abruptly.

Mary looked around Gloria's head and the counter, there was no blood, no sign of injury. Not that she had expected any with the police suspecting an overdose, but after Ethel's murder, she had felt a compulsion to check. Just the note, and one of the pens Mary had seen her packing away yesterday laid across it.

"Ok Mary," Corrigan said. "I think you better leave now. I need to speak to Charles Cotton, and I don't think you should be there."

"Where is he?" she asked, feeling ashamed she had only just thought of him, the shock of Gloria's death having filled her thoughts so wholly.

"He's through the back with two of my officers. I need to go and get an initial statement. If you want to help, you can go and tell the vicar that the funeral's off for today and that one of my officers will be in touch with him about when he can rearrange."

She nodded and stepped out into the street, where a small crowd of villagers were gathered.

Pea and Dot emerged from their centre.

"We got your message," Pea said excitedly. "Is it true? Gloria's dead?"

Mary looked around at the gathered, expectant faces. The news seems to travel around a village-like smoke.

"I don't think we should talk here," she said in a hushed tone.

"Why's that Mary?" A thin, reedy voice came from towards the back of the crowd. People stood aside as the owner of the voice stepped forward. Matt Sharpe was grinning, his eyes fixed on her. "Is it because you saw Gloria Cotton yesterday and apparently had an argument with her? Just like you saw Ethel Long the day before she died? And now the police are letting you go into an active crime scene and traipse about disturbing evidence."

Mary knew from years of experience dealing with the press that they would try to goad you, rile you into saying something that would then be splashed as a headline, and cause you no end of issues when it did. It was best to say nothing, keep your head down, and walk away.

"You're the one trying to profit from other peoples suffering," she snapped back. "You're the one spreading muck and lies about people."

"And you're the one who always seems to be

around when there's a murder." He grinned, before turning back into the crowd.

"Gloria's really dead?" Beryl Copeland stepped forward from the group, her voice cracking with emotion.

Mary knew she couldn't avoid revealing the truth now, not when Gloria's best friend was asking her, tears in eyes. She stepped across to her and took her hands.

"I'm so sorry, Beryl," she said softly.

Beryl burst into tears and turned into the arms of her husband, George, who was staring with narrow eyes at Mary.

"Perhaps you'd like to come back to the vicarage for some tea?" Reggie asked, appearing from their right.

George nodded. "Very kind of you vicar." The three of them moved away.

"Come on," Mary said to Dot and Pea. "I'm sure there's room for a few more."

The crowd watched them go, disappointed now that the entertainment and possibility of more news seemed to be passing.

Mary called after the vicar who turned along with the Copeland's and allowed them to catch up.

"Inspector Corrigan wanted me to tell you that

the funeral will have to be postponed," she said as she reached them.

"Right, of course," he nodded before beginning to turn away.

"I don't suppose we could join you for tea, could we? We've all had a bit of a shock."

The vicar turned to her again, glanced at Dot, and nodded with a smile that seemed less sincere than it had done a few days ago. "Of course."

The six of them walked in silence to the vicarage, where Reggie promptly vanished to make tea along with Dot who asked to help him. Not wanting to leave them alone, Pea quickly followed, and Mary was left with the Copelands who sat huddled on a two-seater sofa.

"I'm so sorry, Beryl, it must be quite a shock."

"I just can't believe it," she said, shaking her head in small, jerky motions.

Mary pursed her lips, knowing that Corrigan would be furious if she gave away too much from the scene, but unable to resist to ask the questions she needed answers to.

"Did you have any indication that Gloria might have been worried about something?" She asked.

"You said she was yesterday, and I knew something wasn't right with her but," she paused and looked up at Mary through tear-filled eyes. "Why are you asking that? Is it something to do with how she died?"

Mary knew she was getting in too deep, but knew she couldn't pull out now.

"The police think she might have taken her own life," she said softly.

"Oh my god," George muttered. "I thought she'd been, you know, killed by the person who killed Ethel."

His wife looked at him in horror.

"Why did you think that?" Mary asked. "Why not an accident or a heart attack or something."

"I don't know," George said wide-eyed.

The others returned with the tea in silence, and Mary saw from their expressions that unpleasant words may well have been exchanged in the kitchen. As Pea and Reggie set down two trays laden with cups, saucers, two teapots, and a plate of biscuits, they became aware of the atmosphere in the room.

"Is everyone ok?" Reggie said, looking at the three of them.

"The police think Gloria bloody topped herself!" George exclaimed as if he could hardly believe it.

"Oh my goodness," the vicar said, swaying slightly and reaching out for the arm of the sofa to support himself.

"She just seems the type," George continued, shaking his head.

"She had her demons," Beryl said in a quiet voice that made everyone e in the room hold their breath to listen. "Times when she'd go all withdrawn and quiet. Ethel's death seemed to upset her something rotten."

"Did you wonder if she had something to do with it?" Mary asked. She immediately felt all eyes in the room turn to her.

"Of course I didn't, why on earth would I?!" Beryl exclaimed.

"Wait," Pea said, midway through his second biscuit even though the tea was as yet to be poured. "Do you mean to say the police think she did?"

"No," Mary lied. "I just wondered if that could have been what drove her over the edge." She turned back to the Copelands who were both staring at her, open-mouthed. "I think it might have been Gloria who had been sending the letters."

"What?!" George barked. "No! It couldn't be!" He turned to his wife. "She wouldn't have done that to us, put us through all of that. She was your friend!"

Beryl just shook her head and stared at the floor, eyes wide.

Dot began pouring the tea, and Mary took the opportunity to eye the vicar's reaction to her news.

He was staring down at the tea set with a vacant expression when he must have sensed her looking at him, and raised his gaze to meet hers.

"Are you saying that Ethel Long didn't send the letters?"

"It seems not," Mary said, enjoying him squirm at the thought. "It just goes to show that people shouldn't throw unsubstantiated rumours around."

He reacted with a worried look, as though she'd slapped him, before replying. "So you think Ethel found out it was Gloria sending the letters, and Gloria killed her?"

"Maybe," Mary said, her eyes boring into his. She was suddenly annoyed at this silly little man. Spreading rumours and lies about Ethel to save his own, thoroughly deserved reputation. He was no different from that bloody reporter Matt Sharpe. She wanted to push him further, make him know how dangerous his games could be. "Or perhaps," she continued, "someone else killed Ethel, thinking she sent the letters, and Gloria couldn't live with the guilt?"

"No, she would have told me," Beryl said in a weak voice.

"I'm sorry Beryl," Mary said, instantly regretting how freely she was throwing theories around in front of people who were grieving. "But if she didn't tell you about the letters, there may be other things she didn't tell you."

"I think I need to have a lie-down," Beryl said, rising from the sofa. Her husband rose with her, and the vicar guided them to the door.

"I think it might be best if you all go," he said to Mary, Dot, and Pea. "I have some things to take care of regarding the funeral cancellation,"

They gave awkward goodbyes and left with only a sip of tea in their stomachs.

CHAPTER TWENTY-SIX

"So what you're telling me," Corrigan said, "is that you've managed to already inform half the village that Gloria Cotton not only wrote the hate mail to everyone but is also almost certainly the killer of Ethel Long?"

"Sort of," Mary said, placing the hand that wasn't holding the phone to her ear to her forehead. "I'm sorry, I know I shouldn't have, but I thought I could find out some more information."

She curled her knees up into the armchair that sat in the library at Blancham hall and sipped at the tea before placing it back on the arm.

"We don't need information Mary, we needed to stay calm and follow protocol. It's pretty clear from the note it was her, and I'm sure we'll find more evidence once the crime lab starts giving me some results, but that doesn't mean we want rumours circulating the village. These places end up making their own version of events like some collective hive mind, and you end up getting the same story from everyone whether it's true or not."

Mary tried not to get cross. She knew Corrigan was right, but after the morning she'd just had, she could do without a lecture.

"Yes, I get it. Thanks," she answered testily. "How is Charles?"

"Pretty shaken up as you could imagine. Claims he had no idea she was the one that had been writing the notes. Also says she's never had any mental health problems, but her writing poison pen letters to half the village suggests he's missed a trick there."

"I'd say so," Mary said, shaking her head. "I still can't believe it."

"Yep, it's a mess, all right. And Mary? There's something else."

Something in his tone made her stomach clench, braced for the bad news.

"That reporter who wrote that article about you?"

"Matt Sharpe?"

"Yes, that's the one. He's been trying to get a comment from my lads all morning. Sounds like he's going to put you right in the middle of all this again."

"What? How?!"

"I think we'll have to wait until tomorrow's Gazette comes out before we know that, but he's been asking about you."

"Oh, great." Mary sighed, taking another sip of tea. She heard Corrigan's breath down the phone and wished she was hearing it through his broad chest, her head resting on it as he embraced her. "Is there any way you can come over later?"

"I'm sorry, I'm going to be on this all night. The boss wants to know why I couldn't find the murderer before she killed herself, which is a fair question, to be honest. I should have gone harder on the Cottons after the husband found the body."

"You don't think he had anything to do with it surely?!"

"Who knows? He was in a state this morning that was real enough, but that doesn't mean he didn't help kill Ethel Long. Maybe he was the ringleader, and that's why his wife killed herself? She couldn't live with the guilt of what he'd made her do?"

Mary tried to picture Charles and Gloria Cotton as some sort of crazed duo. The image didn't fit.

"Do you think he's lying when he said he didn't realise she had written the letters? You think he was involved in that as well?"

Corrigan exhaled in frustration. "No actually, I

could have sworn his shock was genuine. In fact, he flat out refused to believe me until he'd seen the note."

"It was definitely her handwriting, was it?" Mary asked, her mind leaping to a scenario where Gloria's death could have been staged."

"It is. Confirmed by the husband, but we also took some examples from the house. Although I'm no expert, it looks like a match."

"Charles could have forged it, though, he would have known her writing well enough and had examples he could have copied."

"He might have tried, but experts can see hesitations and slight discrepancies when someone has copied someone else's writing. Unless the forger is an expert, but that hardly seems to be likely with Charles Cotton."

"When will you know what killed her?"

"We've got a pretty good idea already."

"What?" Mary asked, surprised that they could have had blood test results so quickly.

"A medication she was on, we found an empty pill bottle behind the counter. Anyway, I've to go. I'll call you tomorrow when I get a moment to breathe."

They said their goodbyes and Mary dropped the phone onto the arm of the chair and cradled her cup of tea.

The case had seemingly come to a conclusion, but it was hardly a satisfying one. Another life had been lost, and there was no one to face justice in a courtroom. She wondered what could possibly have driven Gloria to write the letters in the first place, and then been compelled to cover them up with the murder of Ethel Long. Her mind fell on Ethel now. How had she discovered that Gloria was the author of the letters? Had she confronted Gloria herself rather than go to the police? She certainly had been the type. Mary smiled. Still, though, it was curious that Ethel had found out the author of the letters despite having never received one herself. Mary guessed that it could be put down to the skill she had honed over the years of discovering other people's business.

Then there was Lilly Cooper and the vicar. They had been together on the night Ethel had been killed. Still, Lilly had been driven to the vandalism of the tree just the night before. She was apparently a newly acquired friend of Gloria's. She thought back to her conversation with Gloria just yesterday. She had been sure there was something she had wanted to tell Mary, something that she was holding back about the case. Mary had encouraged her to go to the police, and Gloria had said she couldn't. Was it this conversation that had brought Gloria finally to the edge and then tipped her over until she only saw one way out? Mary shuddered at the thought. It wouldn't do her any good to think like that. She finished her tea and climbed out of the armchair, stretching and headed back into the main house to find some company while trying to ignore the image of Gloria Cotton's eyes that were now burned into her mind. Eyes that were full of regret.

CHAPTER TWENTY-SEVEN

M ary leaned back in her chair, stuffed from the sinfully creamy carbonara that Hetty had just served them all. Pea had called and hired to make dinner again rather than her offering as a friend tonight, claiming that Mary needed it after the day she'd had. Although this might have been true, she suspected that Pea would likely make any excuse to be cooked for by Hetty.

Mary sipped her wine. "Well, I daresay the village will be talking about this for years to come."

They had already covered the events of the day. They had even run through the same thoughts and theories that Mary and Corrigan had run through, but she couldn't entirely move on from the topic just yet.

"They'll definitely be talking about it if Frank

Roach gets his way," Hetty said, rolling her eyes. "He's already putting it about that there might have been something to do with witchcraft involved."

"Really?" Pea said, his long face alighting with interest. "How so?"

"Here, he goes again!" Dot said in a mocking tone.

"He's saying that Gloria must have been possessed somehow and that made her write all those letters and kill Ethel."

"Possessed by who?" Pea asked, oblivious to Dot's tutting.

"It doesn't matter, does it? He's just saying its witchcraft, people can make up their own story. While they're paying for accommodation ale and a reasonably priced meal at The Cauldron of course," she added with a wink.

"He still could have had a motive for all of this," Mary said, more to herself than anything, but realised she had caused the others to focus on her.

"What do you mean?" Pea asked.

"Oh, nothing," Mary said, shaking her head and taking another sip of wine. "I don't know what it is, but I just feel as though this whole thing is unfinished somehow."

"Of course you do," Dot answered, "it *is* unfinished at the moment. We don't know why

Gloria was writing the notes, we don't know how Ethel found out or what happened when she confronted her. We might never know now, but there's nothing more to do."

"I know," Mary said quietly.

"I can see her writing those letters you know," Hetty said for what must have been the fourth time since they had been discussing the case.

"Yes, we know you do Hetty," Pea said with only the merest hint of an eye roll.

"She always had a bit of the devil in her did Gloria."

Mary was reasonably sure that Hetty had never mentioned such a thing before, but hindsight is a powerful thing.

"I tell you one thing though," Hetty continued, "I would never have had her pegged for someone who would kill herself."

"Why do you say that?" Mary asked, sitting upright.

"She just wasn't the type was she?"

"Come on Hetty, you're going to have to give us more than that."

"I'll tell you what Gloria Cotton was: she was a nice enough woman, but she liked to have her little bit of power."

"Actually," Pea said, "I know what you mean.

If I was out when a parcel came, and it ended up at the post office, she'd always make me go through the whole rigmarole of showing my ID to her. Even when she knew perfectly bloody well who I was."

"Exactly!" Hetty said, slapping the table as she warmed to her theme. "She could be petty and like to watch people squirm."

"Which might fit with someone capable of writing those letters," Dot said. "She could have enjoyed the power of it, having half the village talking about whoever was sending them and not knowing it was her."

Pea grinned at her. "Are you hiding some deep desire that we don't know about, Dot?"

"No, I am not," she answered gruffly, but Mary noticed she was stifling a smile and inwardly gave a sigh of relief. It seemed as though things were back on the right track with Dot and Pea.

Hetty gave her a knowing look across the table which she replied with a wink that stayed in place as she suddenly thought of something.

"Charles Cotton received one of the letters."

There was a moment of stunned silence until Mary continued. "She even sent one to her own husband, why would she do that?"

"Maybe that's what this was all about?" Dot said.

Maybe she wanted to get at her husband and so started with him, and then she liked it."

"That sounds like her," Hetty said again.

"You didn't get one, Hetty, and we don't think Ethel Long did either. At least, the police found no evidence of any at her house."

"She'd have had more sense than to send me one," Hetty said proudly. "I'd have given her what for and no mistake."

Mary was in no doubt, this was true. Gloria may well have avoided sending letters to Hetty and Ethel because they were both fearsome characters, but it seemed unlikely. If Dot was right and Gloria had found some kind of pleasure in being an anonymous tormentor, she surely would have revelled in these bigger targets? Was there something else that had prevented her from targeting them?

"Now you mention it," Hetty said in thought as she turned the wine glass in her hand, "Ethel said something odd a few weeks ago about letters. I hadn't thought of it until now..."

"Go on," Mary said expectantly.

"I said I hadn't had a letter that wasn't a bill since Pea here bought me an iPad for my birthday. She said that being the only two tech-minded oldies in the village kept us out of it all."

"What on earth does that mean?" Pea asked.

"Don't ask me," Hetty shrugged, "but Ethel had an iPad like me, and we used to swap tips on using the things when we were both getting started. I remember thinking it was an odd thing to say at the time."

"Of course!" Mary said, her head falling backwards, her eyes closed. "How did we not see it before?!"

"What is it?" Dot asked.

"A small village with an ageing population, what have they pretty much all got in common?"

"Not good at new-fangled technology," Hetty said, proud that she was not included in this bracket.

"Exactly," Mary continued. "Most of the people in Bloxley actually still write letters to people rather than email. Now think, who could easily get her hands on those letters every day?"

"Gloria, who ran the post office!" Pea exclaimed. "Blimey! You think she'd been opening people's mail?!"

Mary frowned at him. "That's not exactly the major crime here is it Pea? You know, what with the poison pen letters and then murdering poor Ethel?"

"No, good point." Pea nodded. "But still, reading other people's mail!"

"It's an outrage!" Hetty agreed, her eyes bright

with indignation. "And just the sort of thing Gloria would do, I always said it!"

Mary rubbed her eyes as exhaustion from the long and eventful day caught up with her like a soft wave rolling across the beach. She drained the last of her wine.

"It's only a theory, but I'm sure we'll find out more tomorrow when the police have had a good look around. I think I'm going to go to bed, leave all this Hetty," she said, gesturing to the plates on the table. "I'll sort it in the morning."

They all gave their goodnights, and she climbed the stairs with leaden feet, forcing her eyes to stay open until her head hit the pillow and she was lost into black.

CHAPTER TWENTY-EIGHT

"You know what they say," Pea said in an entirely unconvincing tone, today's headlines are tomorrow's fish and chip wrappings."

"You do realise who you're talking to don't you? I've had more headlines than you've had successful fishing trips."

"Hey!" Pea said in a hurt voice.

"I'm sorry," Mary said, realising that she had hit Pea where it hurt. "I just can't believe this is happening." She looked down at the headline in front of her again.

MARY BLAKE ON THE SCENE OF ANOTHER MYSTERIOUS DEATH

THE ARTICLE below didn't get any better, just as the last one hadn't. It described how Mary had seen Gloria Cotton the day before she died, just as she saw Ethel. Matt Sharpe, the writer of both articles, had conceded that it sounded like Gloria had taken her own life, but speculated as to whether Mary had in some way caused her to do so.

"Once everything comes out it will be clear you were nothing to do with it, and it will all go away," Dot said.

"Maybe," Mary answered, "but it won't bring Ethel or Gloria back. This happened right on our doorstep, and we didn't manage time stop any of it unfolding."

"It's certainly not going to do the business any good," Pea added glumly. Then, after catching Dot and Mary's looks, added, "but of course, that doesn't matter with what else has happened."

"Of course," Dot repeated, reddening his cheeks further with her disapproving look.

They carried on talking, but Mary's mind had wandered. She was thinking of Gloria Cotton, and the last time she had seen her once again. Why was she finding it so hard to accept that Gloria had done this? She pictured those fearful eyes, but were they afraid of being discovered as the writer of the evil letters that had swept the village and the murderer of Ethel Long? Or was it something else, was it someone else, that had frightened her.

She was snapped from her thoughts by her phone, which buzzed loudly on the table. Corrigan.

"I take it you've seen the paper?" She said, answering and rising from the table as she gestured to the others that she was taking the call elsewhere.

"I've seen it. This Matt Sharpe character is starting to become a pain. Are you sure you don't want me to have a word?"

"No, it's fine. What's the latest with Gloria Cotton?"

"She's definitely the one who wrote the letters. We even found some she hadn't sent yet."

"You know what she was saying to people?"

"We do, and before you ask, I'm not going to repeat it to you, though to be honest there's nothing in there we didn't know already really."

"Right," Mary answered, feeling slightly deflated.

"There is one thing though."

Mary, who had been pacing around the large hallway, paused. "What is it?"

"There's a letter here that looks like it was intended for your brother."

"For Pea?!"

"I'm afraid so, something about a dodgy business deal, but it's only half-written. I'm just giving you a heads up because it's evidence now, someone will be following up on it."

"Right, thanks," Mary said, shocked.

"We haven't got the lab reports back, but the doc says it's likely to have been the blood pressure meds that were missing."

"It was her blood pressure medication?"

Corrigan swore at the other end of the line as he realised he had given away this information.

"I'm too tired to be talking to you, I've been on this all night," he said wearily.

"Go and get some rest, we can talk later."

"Will do, and Mary?"

"Yes?"

"I enjoyed the other night."

Mary smiled as she felt a warm glow rise in her chest. "Me too."

After they had said goodbye, Mary stood for a moment with the phone clutched to her chest. She smiled to herself and pushed the phone back into her pocket as she headed back towards the dining room.

"Any news from the old bill?" Pea asked, smiling.

"Yes actually," Mary said, her expression stopping Pea's smile in its tracks. "The police would like to know about some dodgy business deal you're involved in."

"I knew it!" Dot snapped, rising from the table. The sudden force of her voice made Mary jump as well as Pea. "I said that you were getting into something you were going to regret, you should have just paid for the thing outright!"

Mary's mouth hung open as she stared at her friend. She had rarely seen her this angry. She turned to Pea who had the look of a deer trapped in headlights and waiting for the car to hit. He turned to Mary.

"I don't understand, what did they say? How did they even know about it?!"

"It seems as though Gloria Cotton was about to add you to her correspondence list," Mary answered.

"She was going to write one of those letters to me?"

"She was already writing it, and it mentioned that you were involved in some dodgy deal."

He shook his head and stared down at the table.

"Can someone explain to me hat this is all about?" Mary asked them both. It was Dot who replied.

"Percy here had the great idea of wanting to do something for the village, he wanted to put some money into sprucing up the train station."

"We talked about that," Mary said, looking at her brother.

"I thought we could maybe name it after mum and dad, give them a legacy in the village," he said softly, and Mary felt something lurch in her chest.

"What happened?"

"What happened is that this dope," Dot said, her voice still full of anger, "listened to some conman instead of me!"

Something clicked in Mary's mind. This was the ongoing source of tension between the two of them that had been building over the last few weeks. It may have gone some way to explaining how the appearance of Reggie Downe the vicar had become between them so substantially.

"But who is this person? You didn't give them any money did you, Pea?"

"Of course he did," Dot tutted, "he gave them ten thousand pounds as a deposit."

"A deposit for what?!"

"Who knows!" Dot cried.

Mary could tell this was not about the money. Since they had discovered a long lost Faberge egg that had come into the family's possession many years ago, money was no longer an issue. This was about trust. Dot had warned him not to get involved with whoever this person was, and he had clearly ignored her.

"How did you meet this person?"

"It was someone Beryl Copeland put me on to," Pea said miserably, "but she doesn't seem to know where he is, either. I don't think she really knew him. She'd just heard of him and offered the name up when I asked about having some building work done."

"Pea," Mary said, shaking her head, "not only have you been an idiot, but you should also have mentioned that you'd spoken to Beryl Copeland. Until yesterday she was a potential suspect in a murder!"

"This was months ago," Pea said dismissively. "Anyway, I wasn't the only one to get ripped off by this idiot."

"What?" Dot and Mary said at the same time.

"I had a call from John Cooper late yesterday."

"Lilly's husband?" Mary asked.

"Yes, he said Lily had called him in floods of tears last night after Gloria had been found. Confessed everything to him about her arrest for vandalism, and also that she'd been ripped off by Laslow as well. Mind you, he didn't mention her evening with the vicar, so maybe she wasn't as forthcoming as all that!" He managed a small laugh before his shoulders slumped again. "Bloody hell, it's going to be pretty embarrassing having to talk to the police about this."

"Maybe next time you'll listen to me?" Dot said haughtily.

Pea rose and moved around the table to her. "I will, I promise. Come on Dot, I know you're the one with brains out of us two, I just wanted to do something nice for the village, something for mum and dad."

"I know," Dot said, her voice softening. They moved closer together, and their voices became low.

Usually, Mary would have done the discreet thing and left them to it, but she was deaf to their words and blind to their actions. She was staring, unseeing at the table.

Laslow. That name had rung a bell, and it had stirred something at the back of her mind, and like the bed of a still pond, ripples were forming on the surface as the mud stirred from underneath, clouding the water.

CHAPTER TWENTY-NINE

M ary scrunched up the driveway to Lilly Cooper's house. She had asked Pea and Dot to simply drop her off rather than follow her in as she needed Lilly to be as receptive to talking as possible. She was the kind of woman who spoke more freely one-on-one than when confronted with a group.

After insisting Pea drove her to the village immediately, she had quizzed him on the appearance of the man named Laslow who had seemingly conned him out of a significant amount of money. There was another mystery to unravel here, she was sure of it.

Having given Pea instructions to round Corrigan up and hand him the note she had scrawled out in the car, she leapt out and marched up the driveway to Lilly and John Cooper's house.

Despite her rush to get there, she was unsure how to handle this.

Things hadn't fallen into place for her this morning, the opposite had happened. The neat blocks that held up the wall of this investigation had had one lower block removed. Now the whole thing was teetering, ready to come crashing down around her.

She knew full well what Corrigan would say. He would need proof, evidence. Something that would show him that everything they thought they had known about this case had been wrong. Not only that, but she also needed it for herself. The unease she had had at the idea of Gloria taking her own life now felt a little more real, and the scenario a little more unlikely.

She rang the doorbell and tried to go through what she was going to say in her mind.

When Lilly answered, she looked surprised to see her.

"Oh, Mary."

"Hi Lilly, I was just wondering if I could have a quick word?"

"Um, ok," she answered in her shy, quiet voice. She stepped back and guided Mary through to the hallway and then into the large sitting room she had been in previously.

"Can I get you a drink or anything?"

"No, no, I'm fine," Mary said, taking the seat that was offered to her.

She looked properly at Lilly for the first time. It was obvious she had been crying. Her eyes were still ringed with telltale puffy darkness.

"Lilly, I'm sorry about Gloria, I know you and her were close."

Lilly nodded as she bit her top lip. For a moment, she thought she might burst into tears right there and then, but instead, she spoke in her quiet, mouse-like voice.

"I thought she had been very kind to me, I just can't believe that she would do this."

Right, Mary thought. So the village grapevine had already got the word around that Gloria was the phantom letter writer. She was glad she had spilt the beans to the vicar and the Copeland's. Even if it had annoyed Corrigan.

"You mean the letters?"

"Yes, the letters!" she squeaked suddenly. "She was pretending to be my friend, her and Beryl letting me into their little group, and all the time she was laughing at me behind my back! Maybe they both were?"

She was angry now, and her doll-like face was pink with emotion.

"You think Beryl was in on the letter writing as well?"

"I don't know," she sagged. "Those two were thick as thieves, everyone said so." She looked at Mary now with large, sad eyes that were rimmed with tears. "I was just so lonely with John being away so much. I was so desperate to fit in."

Mary's pulse quickened as she sensed that Lilly was opening up.

"Gloria was so nice to me," She said again.

"And Beryl?" Mary asked.

Lilly looked up at her. "That's what makes all this so horrible, Beryl was so upset about the letters and Gloria never said a word. She must feel so awful now, finding out her friend was lying to her all this time."

Some of the tension left Mary's body. She was right.

"Lilly," Mary said in a calm tone, "was it really you who burnt those words into the lightning tree?"

Her wide eyes blinked back at her for a moment before she nodded with a small, quiet. "Yes."

"The thing is Lilly, I don't think I believe you," Mary continued, causing Lilly recoil in shock. "At least, I don't think you could have done it alone."

Mary leaned forward in her chair as she sensed a slight start from Lilly as she said this. "Was there someone else with you that night Lilly? It's important."

Lilly swallowed. "Beryl was there with me," she said quietly. Mary had to restrain herself despite her growing excitement. If she pushed Lilly too hard, she'd undoubtedly go back into her shell.

"I get it," Mary said in a soft, friendly voice. "Beryl was so upset by the letters and you wanted to help her somehow. To make the letters stop. You both thought it was Ethel who was writing them, so you decided to scare her off."

"I thought it was too much, but Beryl said Ethel would never stop if we didn't frighten her a bit. I felt just awful about it afterwards."

"But you had received letters as well, you had a right to be angry. It's understandable you might want some sort of revenge."

"It's silly, now I think about it," Lilly said with a small laugh. "I made a mistake and lost some money and was just so worried about telling John that I didn't know what to do when the letters started coming. But I should have known he would be absolutely fine about it. I spoke to him today, and he was so understanding." She smiled softly. "He's so kind."

"I know it's hard," Mary said, ignoring the rather rosy image Lilly had of her husband, "but was the financial trouble you had something to do with the building work you were having done here?"

Lilly grimaced, "Yes. How did you know?"

"I think my brother was stung by the same person. Was his name Laslow?"

Mary held her breath as she waited for Lilly's response, but it was clear from the rising of her eyebrows that there was recognition there.

"Yes, yes, it was! I'm sorry to hear about your brother, but I have to say, it does make me feel a little better to know I wasn't the only one fooled by him. He gave me such a good price on renovating the stonework, but once he'd set up the bit of scaffolding outside, he said he needed an advance for materials. That it would be cheaper if we bought now in bulk." She gave a small sigh. "I never saw him again and the number he gave me just rings out."

"And was it Beryl who introduced you to him?"

Lilly frowned. "Beryl? Why on earth would she have introduced him to me? She didn't even know about it until afterwards."

"But you did tell her after it had happened?"

"Yes. I'm sorry, but I don't understand."

"We think Gloria found out information to use in

the letters by opening people's mail in the post office."

"Oh my goodness!" Lilly said, her hand moving to her mouth.

"Did you have any correspondence through the post with Laslow?"

"No, I...I see what you mean. How did Gloria know? I didn't tell her!"

"But you told Beryl?"

"Yes." She said, her breathing becoming more rapid. "So they were in on it together! But that doesn't make sense! Beryl couldn't have been pretending to be upset, she just couldn't have!"

"Maybe she wasn't," Mary said, her mind racing.

"What?"

"Maybe Beryl didn't know it was Gloria sending the letters either." Her eyes focused on Lilly again. "At least, not at first."

"Well," Lilly said determinedly, "I'm going to have it out with her when she gets here."

"When she gets here?" Mary said, her voice rising.

"Yes, she called earlier and said she needed to talk to me. She said that we needed to stick together after what had happened with Gloria and yet she was the one who told her about my money problems!"

"Lilly," Mary said urgently. "You need to tell me exactly what happened on the night of the murder."

"You don't still think I had something to do with it, do you? I told you I have an alibi!"

"Yes," Mary said with meaning, "the vicar."

Lilly looked shocked. "You know I was with Reggie?!"

"Yes," Mary said with meaning.

"Nothing happened, you know!" Livvy said urgently. "There's nothing going on between us!"

"But you were with him the night Ethel was killed?"

"Yes, until it was light. We were just talking, there was nothing funny going on though! We were just talking!" She closed her eyes and took a deep breath. "I just needed someone to talk to, and he was so kind."

I bet he was, thought Mary.

The doorbell chimed, and they both jumped in their seats.

"That will be Beryl." Lilly said it in a matter of fact way, but her eyes betrayed her concern. She rose from her chair and moved towards the door before pausing and turning back to Mary. "You won't tell her I thought she might have had something to do with the letters, will you?"

Mary looked at her nervous face and realised that

Lilly was back to worrying that Beryl wouldn't allow her into the village clique. She wasn't harbouring the growing concerns that Mary was about Beryl Cotton.

"Yes, fine," Mary answered with a smile.

The moment she had left the room, Mary pulled her phone from her pocket and began furiously typing a message as she listened to Lilly opening the front door and pleasantries being given.

She had just finished shoving the phone back into her pocket as the door to the sitting room was pushed open again. Lilly entered first, looking slightly confused and worried, with Beryl close behind her.

"Mary," she said with a smile, "this is a pleasant surprise."

CHAPTER THIRTY

L illy hurried out to make them all tea, and Beryl and Mary stared at each other from across the room. Mary was seated on one of the two sofas which faced each other across the heavy coffee table. Beryl stood behind the sofa opposite her, arms folded.

"Lilly tells me that you've been talking about Gloria?"

"That's right." Mary nodded but didn't expand further.

"It's all deeply upsetting of course," Beryl continued in a flat tone that didn't match her words. "That she would take her own life like that."

"I'd imagine it's not as upsetting as finding out she was the one behind the letters?"

A flicker of something passed across Beryl's face and was gone again in an instant.

"Yes, well maybe sometimes people who play with fire can get burnt," she said, her voice hard.

"That's not what happened to Ethel though, was it?" Mary said.

This time there was a different reaction. The colour drained from Beryl's face, all traces of the hard bitterness that had been creeping into her voice, gone. "No," she said quietly.

"Ethel was killed because the whole village thought she was the one behind the letters, thanks to the vicar."

"It wasn't the vicar's fault," Beryl said quickly. "Gloria knew the whole time and didn't say a thing! She just sat there while it all got stirred up around Ethel and let it all happen!"

"I'm sure she never dreamed that you would go far enough as to kill Ethel for it, though."

The words fell into the space between them like small explosive devices that seemed to suck all the air from the room.

"Right, here's the tea," Lilly said, appearing through the doorway with a tray. She hesitated for a moment as she saw the gaze of both Mary and Beryl locked with each other, and then promptly broke it by placing the tray down on the coffee table between them and began busying herself laying out the cups and saucers.

"I was introduced to someone the other day by your husband Beryl," Mary said, "Your cousin, Phillip Laslow."

Lilly dropped the cup she had been placing in front of Mary, causing it to roll off the table and land with a dull thud in the soft carpet. She stood upright with both hands rushing to her mouth.

"You did know him!" she cried, waving an accusing finger at Beryl. "Mary said you did but I didn't think you would be involved in stealing from me!"

Beryl looked back to Mary in surprise, rose, and moved across to the fireplace where she leaned on the mantelpiece and looked out of the rear french doors at the far end of the long room which led onto the garden. After a moment, she turned back towards Lilly.

"This is just as much of a shock for me as it is for you, Lilly. When you said the man who had run off with your deposit was called Laslow, I had no idea it was my cousin!"

"Oh come on," Mary said. "You even gave his name to my brother to pull the same stunt! I wonder just how many times you and your cousin have worked together on things like this?"

"You told Gloria about it," Lilly continued in a shaky voice. "You and her were writing the letters together and laughing at me behind my back!"

"No!" Beryl shouted, suddenly angry. "That bitch wrote those letters herself, and do you know why? Do you know why she caused misery and worry and panic in half the village? Because she was bored, that's what she told me!"

Something had snapped in Beryl at the mention of Gloria and the letters. She was ranting now, and Mary hoped and prayed that Lilly would keep her mouth shut and let her continue.

"She was bored with the village, bored with her fussy little husband, and bored with running the shop. So she played with all our lives like it was some sort of sick game. She got pleasure every time she saw that someone was worried by her poisonous letters. She told me that! Actually told me." She spat the words incredulously.

"Right there with tears streaming down her face, crying for poor old Ethel. As if she suddenly gave a crap about anyone!" She began to mimic a high pitch, pathetic version of Gloria's voice. "I never thought anyone would get hurt, how was I to know this would happen?" She shook her head and gripped the mantelpiece, breathing hard. "The stupid cow didn't even realise she was telling the one person she shouldn't have."

"Because you killed Ethel," Mary said, causing Lilly to give a small gasp to her left. "You were so full of anger about the letters, which I'd guess in your case, exposed your little schemes with your cousin? For you to react as you did, I'd imagine my brother and poor Lilly here aren't the only people you've scammed. So you killed Ethel. I don't know how you lured her out to the tree at night to do it. Maybe you teased her with some information? Or just said you needed help? Whatever it was, it worked. Of course, you chalked some strange looking symbols on her afterwards, not because it was anything to do with witchcraft, but because it was a distraction. That's why you convinced Lilly to vandalise the tree the night before, you thought it would cause enough confusion around the murder that the inevitable investigation would be thrown off."

Mary had been winging it, her thoughts tumbling from her mouth as soon as her mind had formed them. From the look on Beryl's face, she was sure she was on the right track, but now something else had occurred to her. She glanced at Lilly. "Actually, I wonder if it wasn't just a distraction. Maybe you were planning on setting Lilly up for the murder? She may well have told the police you were involved in the vandalism eventually, but would they believe her by then if they thought she was the killer? I wonder if you kept some key piece of evidence back from that night that you were going to implement her with later? There was a problem though, she had an alibi for the night of the murder. One that you knew nothing about."

She turned to Lilly. "The night Ethel was killed, you were with the vicar. Did Beryl know that?"

Lilly shook her head and then spoke, her voice just a squeak. "No, we'd arranged to meet, but Beryl cancelled at the last minute."

Mary gave a humourless laugh. "So she arranged to meet you to make sure you were free and at home alone that night so that you wouldn't have an alibi. She didn't realise you'd made other plans afterwards."

Mary turned back to Beryl, who was staring at her with a steely, unreadable expression. Mary knew she had to buy time.

"It must have been quite a shock when the police released Lilly and only charged her for the vandalism, but I'm guessing not quite as big as when you talked to Gloria a few days later. How did it happen, exactly? I know she was in a state over Ethel's death. Not surprising, really. As you said, Beryl, she must have thought of the letters as a kind of game, a harmless bit of fun. She never expected someone to actually die. I'd imagine she was wracked with guilt and just blurted it all out to you. You were, after all, her closest friend." Mary shook her head. "You must have been furious. She'd lied to you all this time and had driven you to murder an innocent woman, and now she wanted your pity, she wanted your help. You showed self-control, though. You knew if you killed her in the same way you had with Ethel you'd only be increasing your chances of being caught. You had to think. You had to find a way of getting the revenge you needed."

"It wasn't just revenge for me!" Beryl said, cutting her off in a low, stiff voice that felt full of tension. "It was for everyone she sent letters to. For everyone who's lives she thought she could just play with like they were all just there for her amusement. And it was for Ethel." Her voice was shaking with emotion now. "She made me kill her, it was her!"

She had screamed these last words, her face twisted in fury as she reached down and picked up the long, black metal poker that had hung by the fire.

CHAPTER THIRTY-ONE

M ary's gaze moved to the poker as though
magnetised. She followed its black shaft
until it came to a dull point, with another curling into
a hook below it. Mary thought of Ethel Long, and the
blow she had taken to the head. She was in no doubt
that Beryl was capable of dealing her a similar fate.
She needed to keep her talking.

"I still don't understand how you managed to get
Beryl to take an overdose of medication?" Mary said.
"Or how you got her to write her suicide note?"

"Maybe she really did kill herself?" Beryl
laughed with a tilt of her head. Her face was changed
now. The plain butcher's wife was gone and had now
been replaced by something vile. A grimace of
grotesque pain and anger.

"I don't think so," Mary said in a steady voice. "I think you did something very clever, tricked her somehow?"

"Ha!" Beryl snarled. "You make it sound like it was hard! Gloria never was the sharpest tool in the shed. All I had to do was tell her we would work it out together. I told her she needed to go to the police and that she should write it all down and get her story straight."

Mary thought back to the letter she had read. A confession to writing the letters, and then just the sentence that was left unfinished

I'm so sorry about Ethel, but

"I interrupted her at the right moment and gave her a little pick-me-up drink. Well, that's what I told her it was."

"But how did you manage to crush her medication into her drink without her noticing?" Mary asked.

"I didn't," Beryl smiled.

Instead of offering any further explanation, she took a step away from the fireplace and towards them. Lilly instinctively stepped back but was halted by a shout from Beryl.

"Don't move Lilly," she snapped. "We're going to

have to think of a way out of this, you and I." She was fixing Lilly with her gaze as she took another step towards her on the far side of the coffee table from Mary.

"Mary is going to want to go to the police with all this, and it will get messy for us. You don't want to be all over the national press for being involved in all this, do you? What would John say about that? I doubt his company would be too happy with the publicity. Maybe he'd even lose his job?"

Mary watched Lilly's face that was frozen in horror.

"You and I can sort all this out, then you and John can get on with your lives. Mary can just have had an accident. She was ranting, raving about all sorts of theories and she attacked you. I came to help, and she hit her head on the fireplace, that' all. It will be easy."

"My god, you're insane!" Mary cried, but she failed to wrest Beryl's gaze away from Lilly.

"Don't listen to her," Beryl continued, "she's an actress, she lies for a living! She doesn't care about you, not like I do. We were becoming friends, weren't we, you and I?"

Beryl inched closer to Lilly, and Mary knew she had to do something soon. If she didn't, Beryl was either going to attack Lilly or, less likely, convince her that they should both deal with Mary.

Mary glanced around her, but the only thing she could see was the teapot that still stood untouched on the coffee table. Beryl was right behind it: if Mary made a move for it, the poker raised in her hands would come crashing down on Mary's skull before she could do anything. Then, with a rush of adrenaline, Mary realised what she had to do. It would be a risk, but to do nothing would end badly for either her or Lilly. She had to act now.

"Do it with me," Beryl said to Lilly.

And Mary kicked hard at the edge of the coffee table nearest to her, slamming it forward into Beryl's legs. She was knocked sprawling onto the sofa on the opposite side as crockery smashed at her feet.

Mary leapt up from her seat and caught the teapot just before it slid off the edge and brought it down had on Beryl's head, causing her to slump backwards, eyes closed.

It didn't break, but the solid thunk as it connected reassured Mary that she would be out for a while. She snatched the crowbar away from her, just in case, and turned to Lilly, who was shaking like a leaf.

She moved to her and put her arms around her as Lilly descended into loud sobs.

There was a sudden, frantic noise from the hallway and Corrigan burst in, eyes wide, followed by Dot and Pea.

"About bloody time!" Mary said, trying to keep the tremor from her voice.

CHAPTER THIRTY-TWO

M ary laughed so hard an unexpectedly she actually snorted.

"I mean it," Corrigan continued. "We should get in touch with the world record people." He held his hand up in front of him and moved it along as he spoke, as though reading a headline "'World's first arrest via teapot', it's got a great ring to it."

"I'm just glad I didn't accidentally kill her," Mary said when she'd finally stopped laughing at the absurdity of it all.

They were standing in the hall at Blancham, Corrigan's arms around her waist. She felt ludicrously happy. Giddy with the euphoria of surviving a dangerous situation, solving the case. Now Corrigan had come, and it was like a wall that had been between them was suddenly crumbling.

"Ah, ha!" Pea cried from behind her, emerging from the dining room with Dot. "What news, Inspector?" Pea said with a grin.

"She's not talking," Corrigan said, pulling away from Mary slightly to address him. "But we don't need her to now."

"You found hard evidence?"

He smiled. "Remember in your statement? You said you'd asked her how she had managed to spike Gloria Cotton's drink without her knowing?"

"Yes?"

"We think she brought it with her."

Mary frowned. "But then how did she get the..." She paused, remembering something George Copeland had said when she had been in the butcher's shop, 'it's not doing Beryl's blood pressure any good'.

"She was on the same blood pressure medication!" She exclaimed.

"Almost the same," Corrigan answered, "and that's where we've got her. We think she pre-made this 'pick-me-up' she'd made for Gloria at home. She's known for it by all accounts. She ground her pills in it and covered the taste with blended fruit and some Tobasco. Then she took it over when they met in the middle of the night. Charles Cotton is a heavy sleeper and didn't even know his wife had gone downstairs until the morning."

"But didn't you find Gloria's pillbox empty next to her? Where did those pills go? Actually, now I think about it. Why did she have her pillbox with her at all? Beryl can't have got it."

"Think about it," Corrigan said playfully. He looked across the three of them. "You three are detectives, aren't you?"

Mary thought about Corrigan's earlier words. They had found some evidence, but what could it be? If they knew Beryl had taken her pills to Gloria, then they might have seen her empty bottle at her house, but then where did Gloria's pills go? She realised with a start.

"You checked Beryl's pill bottle, and it was full, but the pills were a different dosage!" She cried.

"Exactly," Corrigan smiled. He leaned forward and kissed her forehead. Mary realised that just a few months ago she may well have slapped anyone who tried to do something so condescending, but now, she only felt an increasingly familiar warm glow spread through her.

"Beryl took her pills, ground them up, and gave them to Gloria. We're not sure exactly how, but she persuaded Gloria to bring her medicines down when they met. She probably said she was running out herself and needed to borrow some or something. In any case, once Gloria had died, she poured her pills into her own box and took them home. She must have known she might end up a suspect and we'd check whether her pills were missing, and so she'd replaced them. She didn't pay enough attention to the strength, though."

"And you think that will be enough to convict?" Dot asked.

"Along with the testimony of Mary and Lilly Cooper, we think so. We're also uncovering considerable financial irregularities. We've picked up her cousin, Phillip Laslow, and he seems like he might talk."

"Good," Pea said firmly. "The bloody rotter!"

"We might need you to give evidence against him," Corrigan said.

"Right," Pea said reddening. "I guess if you do something stupid, you need to own up to it, I'll do it."

"We were just off out for a walk if you want to join us?" Dot asked. "We thought we'd walk down to the train station and look again at what could be done for the place. You know, without handing money over to a conman." She smiled at Pea impishly, causing him to roll his eyes.

"Mary looked at Corrigan, "We'll catch you up."

Mary and Corrigan just looked at each other as

the others gathered their coats and headed out of the large front door.

"You know Mary Blake," Corrigan said in a low voice, "you are a remarkable woman."

Mary smiled.

"And it's nice to finally see you."

She gave him a quizzical look. "You saw me just yesterday!"

"No," he said, bringing her closer to him, his hand reach up and pushing a stray strand of hair from her face. "It's nice to finally see you."

MORE FROM A.G. BARNETT

Brock & Poole Mysteries

An Occupied Grave

A Staged Death

When The Party Died

Murder in a Watched Room

The Mary Blake Mysteries

An Invitation to Murder

A Death at Dinner

Lightning Strikes Twice

For news on upcoming books and special offers, visit
agbarnett.com

MAILING LIST

Get FREE SHORT STORY *A Rather Inconvenient Corpse* by signing up to the mailing list at agbarnett.com